EASY TO LOSE

S.A. CLAYTON

S.A. CLAYTON

MORGAN

FOUR MONTHS EARLIER

"Where's this elusive fiancé you've been hiding from us?" Claire jokes, placing a party hat on top of my head and ignoring my eye roll. I can feel the anger start in my fingertips as I grip the glass in my hand, tighter and tighter. Aaron promised he'd be here. He also promised that he'd make an effort this year.

And yet… He's not here.

As I look across the room, I see a group of people making their way into the space, and for a split second, I hope he's one of them. But as the last person enters, and it's not my fiancé, I wonder if he'll show up at all.

"Why is this thing on my head?" I ask, taking a sip

of the champagne someone handed me when I walked into the room. The space is gorgeous, which I knew it would be since it's one of my favorite restaurants in New York City. The place is filled with gold and silver streamers, and there's confetti on every table. To be honest, it looks like New Year's Eve threw up in here, and I fucking love it. Even though it's July—a full six months after the *actual* holiday—I still smile when I look around.

"Morgan, it's your birthday. You'll do as I say since I planned this whole thing, and you should be grateful!" I smirk at her, knowing she's right and loving her for setting this up. "But enough about the party, stop changing the subject!" she says, smacking my arm.

I haven't known Claire long, but she's quickly become one of my closest friends. On my first day at the Bloomingdales head office, she selflessly warned me about a rogue coffee machine that spat coffee every time you pressed a button, and we've been best friends ever since.

"I'm not changing the subject. I'm just refusing to answer it," I admit, quickly glancing at my watch and feeling the pit in my stomach start to expand. It's already after nine o'clock, and the party started almost two hours ago. He should be here by now.

I look at the platinum ring on my left hand, wondering where he could be. He knows that tonight isn't just about my birthday party, it's about finally introducing him to my friends—something we've talked about for months.

"I'm just saying, it's after nine, and the party is dwindling." Her gaze leaves mine to move around the room, watching as people say their goodbyes. "Maybe you should call him? See where he is." I nod absently, taking my phone out of the back pocket of my skin-tight black jeans and going out onto the restaurant's terrace. Once outside, the noise of the city blocks out the din of the party as I press Aaron's name and listen to the phone ring, and ring. And ring. After a few more tries, I take a deep breath and head back inside. The worry demons inside my head run rampant as possible scenarios play out. *Has he been in an accident? Is he okay? Is he dead somewhere, and I'll never find him?*

Yet an annoying little voice residing in the back of my head thinks he's perfectly fine, simply being the Aaron I've slowly started to dislike. It's been a gradual change, and at times I wonder if I'm over-thinking his behavior. But then he does things like this, and I go back to being pissed.

"No luck?" Claire asks as I make my way back

into the room. I shake my head, putting my phone into my pocket, trying to shake the uneasy feeling crawling all over my skin. I look around and notice that most of the guests have headed home. I'm not naïve to the fact that we're older now and staying out past ten isn't exactly a good thing for most adults, especially when you have to work the next day.

I take off the party hat, set down my champagne glass, and take Claire's hand. "I think I'm gonna head out." I'm trying to stay strong but the look in her eyes tells me she sees the unshed tears wanting to fall and knows I need to be alone. So, she just gives me a hug and a sad smile before letting me walk out the door.

AARON and I met while I was on a business trip in Connecticut last year. We were staying at the same hotel and saw each other every morning before we went our separate ways. We started having breakfast together, and that turned into lunch and then dinner. Eventually, when it was time for us to go home, we promised that we would stay in touch.

I can't lie and say the long-distance relationship didn't have its challenges—sex being the biggest one

—but we made it work. Then I got the news about Bloomingdales wanting a new head buyer and knew it was my shot. And the fact that Aaron was also in New York was the icing on the cake.

Everything was falling into place, almost like it was meant to be.

But after he proposed a few weeks ago, everything started to change for some reason. He's almost never home on time, he works constantly, and our sex life has taken a dive into the gutter. I try not to overthink it because one should never believe the voices in their head, but tonight, those voices are a lot louder than normal.

Walking up to our brownstone and standing in front of the door with the keys in my hand, I freeze. The cool summer breeze brushes across the exposed parts of my skin, sending a shiver through my entire body. I don't know what makes me pause, but for a split second, I wonder if I should stay at Claire's house, talk to Aaron in the morning, and let myself cool down. Because if he's not dead in a ditch somewhere, he might be soon if I find him in this house when he should have been with me.

I open the door, noticing that the kitchen light is on down the hall. Not necessarily uncommon, but it still makes the anger boil a little faster inside my veins. *He's home? Probably fucking sleeping while I was waiting for him at my own birthday party. The man is dead.*

I set my purse on the dining room table to my right and make my way down the hall. I think about calling his name but decide against it. Instead, I head into the kitchen to get myself a glass of wine. I feel my phone vibrate in my pocket and take it out to see a text from Claire, telling me she hopes I had a good birthday despite Aaron's lack of tact. I smile and text her back, saying that she made the day better just by being by my side. I smile at the heart eyes emoji she replies with. I'm just about to send one back when I enter the kitchen and stop dead in my tracks.

Because there, standing buck-naked in our kitchen, is my dear fiancé with a leggy brunette, her legs wrapped around his hips, moaning his name as he pistons into her like it's an Olympic sport. It takes a second for my brain to catch up to my eyes, but when it does, the anger that I felt earlier boils over and starts to turn into blinding pain. But I push the hurt down and focus on the rage. It will get me through this.

"Ahem!" I say, clearing my throat, crossing my arms over my chest and jutting out a hip. It takes a second for Aaron to hear me, but his whole body locks when he does.

"Fuck!" Aaron sputters as his eyes meet mine, and he oh-so-graciously stops fucking the woman wrapped around him.

"Why are you stopping, baby…that felt so good!" The brunette moans as she reaches for him. But his eyes never leave mine, and before long, her head finally turns my way, her eyes bulging with surprise. "I thought you said she would be out all night!"

I roll my eyes at the cliché in front of me, but inside? Inside, I'm dying. The girl that was so excited about finding a guy who loved her for her and not the size of her hips? *That* girl is devastated that her dream is now a nightmare.

Before I can stop them, the tears start to fall, trailing down my cheeks, streaking the makeup I worked hours to perfect. My fingers angrily wipe them away as I turn and make my way to our bedroom. Or is it only mine now? Or is it his? I have no fucking idea what to do in this situation. Do I stay and talk it out?

No.

I shudder at the thought of talking about this night. Ever. So I resign myself to packing up whatever I can fit into a suitcase and calling Claire. In the back of my mind, I know the sensible thing to do is leave. Not pack everything, just go. But I can't. All I want to do is pack up everything I can possibly cram into this damn suitcase so I don't have to come back here tomorrow and see his face.

"Morgan!" Aaron calls from down the hall, and I just start throwing things into the bag, not worrying about folding. I need to get out of this house. I head into the bathroom and gather everything that's mine. My eyes catch on a glint from the ring on my finger, and suddenly I'm on the floor in front of the toilet, food and booze making a second appearance. This was not how tonight was supposed to go.

After I gather myself, I get up off the floor, rinse out my mouth, and eye the ring again. Before I think better of it, I toss it into the toilet and flush, watching the future I thought I'd have go down the drain. Just as I gather my things and head into the bedroom, the door bursts open, and I do everything I can to avoid looking in Aaron's direction. I just continue going through drawers and throwing shit on top of the bed.

"Morgan stop. Let's talk about this…" His voice is calm, and before I can think better of it, my eyes land on him. The regret is instantaneous. His shaggy brown hair is a mess as if someone's been running their fingers through it for hours.

Her fingers.

THE DARK BROWN of his eyes looks right through me as I feel his stare down to my bones. He's always had a knack for making me surrender with just a look, and I have to actively stop myself from caving because his eyes have always been my weakness. His shirt is still missing, and his jeans hang loosely from his hips, unbuttoned and barely zipped. But what gets me are the lipstick stains on his perfectly carved chest.

"Talk? You seriously want to talk to me, looking like that?" I point at the offending marks as he rolls his eyes, taking a step toward me as I take one back. "No. you don't get to do that anymore. You lost the right to come anywhere near me when you stuck your dick in her!" I scream, pointing at the door, referring to the girl that I hope is long gone.

"Morgan, we can fix this." I shake my head. He's clearly delusional.

"No. I'm done. Seeing you with her after you promised to spend the rest of your life with *me*? I'm never going to un-see that, Aaron. Never."

"Don't be melodramatic. We can get through this. I just needed one last night of bachelorhood before we got married. That's all. It's common to get cold feet, right?" I can't help but laugh. That is by far the most self-centered thing he could have said. And by the look on his face, I can see he meant every word, too.

"'Cold feet' does not give you permission to stick your dick in any waiting snatch you can find." I feel the tears start once again, and take a deep breath, steeling myself for what I need to do. "Now, if you'll excuse me…" I throw the rest of my stuff into the suitcase and zip it up, carrying it out of the room and down the hall, hearing his steps following mine the entire way.

"Morgan, stop this. If it weren't for me, you would still be a sad, lonely, fat girl who'd never even had a guy go down on her." I stop in my tracks, staring at the front door, and the first steps to my life away from this nightmare. "You know you need me. You know that, without me, you are nothing." The words cut deeper than I want, but I straighten my back, turn my head, and look straight at him.

"I'm leaving."

I don't look back again as I step outside and slam the door behind me. My steps don't waver as I walk to my car and get in, but when the door shuts, and the silence surrounds me? I start to crack. The solid veneer I created the moment I saw Aaron with that woman crumbles and

I finally let the tears fall, wondering what my life has become, and what the hell I'm going to do now.

2

MORGAN

*P*resent Day

It's fucking sweltering. Something I seem to have forgotten as I set the last box on my living room floor and look around my new house. Growing up in Miami, you get used to the weather. But being away for ten years? It seems you forget that the only seasons are hot, hot as hell, and hot with a side of hurricanes. Am I going to miss the leaves changing in October? Of course. Fall was my favorite part of New York City. Will I miss the winter? Hell, no.

"You all set?" my dad asks from the doorway. I turn and smile as he watches my mom putter around the kitchen, putting away all my dishes and cutlery. "Diana, honey, I think Morgan can do that herself."

Mom just rolls her eyes and goes back to taking each plate, rinsing it in the sink, and then putting it away just the way she likes. I think we all know that I'll change it all when she leaves, but knowing she's happy right now while organizing my kitchen? It makes it all worth it.

"Dad, you know she's not leaving until it's all done."

"I know." He sighs, coming over to wrap an arm around my shoulder. "I was just hoping to catch the end of the game."

"You better not be complaining about missing that football game, James Lawson!" Mom yells from the kitchen, and Dad just puts his index finger to his mouth, telling me to keep quiet.

Laughing, I go back to the front door and out to the truck to ensure there's nothing left.

"You know we're happy to have you home, honey," Dad says, leaning against the side of the truck. I nod, knowing he and Mom are ecstatic that I decided to move back. "I want to kill that bastard," he grumbles almost too low for me to hear, but I do anyway. I hide my smile as a warm feeling fills my chest.

"Me, too," I whisper as our eyes meet, a small smirk tracing the edges of his lips. "But it's over, and

I'm determined to leave all of that behind me. That's why I'm here...*and* because I was offered a job." Dad laughs lightly as he takes the last bag out of the back of his truck, and we head inside once more.

"I always did like that Allie Baker. She always seemed to have a good head on her shoulders, especially for someone with that much family money."

"Dad!" I say, swatting his arm, hating that people always look at the Bakers with dollar signs in their eyes when they are some of the nicest and most welcoming people you will ever meet. Granted, I've only met them a handful of times, but from what I've seen, the money is second to taking care of their family.

"What? They have money, lots of it. And for some people, that changes the way they treat others. I'm just pointing out that it hasn't changed her." I give him a sideways look and walk into the kitchen just as Mom puts the last of the plates away.

"All done, Mom?" She turns and gives me her signature smile that she passed down to me, along with her blond hair and a dusting of freckles. She's petite, something I did not inherit, and only stands about five feet tall. I, on the other hand, got Dad's height, along with his build. A curse growing up, and something that still lingers on the periphery, no matter how hard I try and embrace the body I was born with.

"Yeah, sweetie, I think we'll leave you to do the rest." I give her a small smile, relieved that I'll have some time to myself. "You are always welcome to come over. Anytime." She kisses my cheek, hugging me too tightly, but I absorb it all since it's been so long since I was last home. "I left some food in the freezer. All you need to do is put it into the oven for an hour," she whispers as Dad takes her hand and leads her to the front door.

"Thanks, Mom, I've missed your cooking," I say as they wave goodbye on their way out. Dad's trusty Ford pickup backs up, and I laugh as it backfires, scaring the neighbors sitting on their porch across the street. Dad has had that truck since I was a teenager and refuses to get a new one. He says he'll drive it until something important falls off or it catches on fire. I hope for the former.

I head back inside, shut the door, and for the first time since I moved in, silence surrounds me as I lean my head back against the wood. Who would have thought I would be starting over at twenty-eight, leaving what I thought was my dream job and moving home to partner with my college roommate?

I look around the room and take stock of the

space, knowing it'll take me at least the weekend to unpack all the boxes. I groan at the prospect of organizing all my stuff. I've never been a clean person, but I vow right here and now to make an effort...or at least a conscious choice to keep this place looking like an actual adult lives here.

IT'S BEEN hours since my parents left, and it doesn't even look like I made a dent in the pile of boxes surrounding me. Maybe that's because with every one I open, I decide to go down the rabbit hole and look at every piece of crap that's in there. There's a memory box open on the floor now, pictures scattered everywhere, and a new pile of them in my hand. I don't know what made me open this or decide to go through the memories that I would rather forget, but here I am.

High school is never a fun time, at least not for anyone but the popular kids, and I can say right now that I was *not* a popular kid. At that time, I was starting to gain weight, I didn't know how to do my hair or makeup, and I was so painfully shy that the thought of talking to anyone made me want to hurl.

The picture in my hand makes me smile, though,

as I remember the day it was taken. It's of me and my best friend, Owen, as we went out for Halloween one year. He's dressed as a dead hockey player, and I'm decked out as a dead hippie. We were probably too old to trick-or-treat but dressing up and walking around with him made the problems in my life seem minuscule. The name-calling, the whispers, and the laughter at my expense all went away when I was with Owen. We were inseparable…until senior year, when everything changed. *He* changed.

My phone vibrates next to me. I read the name and smile, bringing it to my ear to answer. "Hey, Allie," I say, putting all the pictures back inside the box and hoping the weighted memories of my past start to fade.

"I hope you're ready for tomorrow!" she yells as I get up off the floor and make my way into the kitchen. I roll my eyes as she continues. "Don't roll your eyes at me, woman! I know you just got there and are probably tired, but come on! New store! New beginning!" Her enthusiasm is contagious, and I can't help the smile that crosses my face. Tomorrow we start construction, something that both excites and terrifies me.

"I am very tired," I admit, fighting off a yawn as I get myself a glass of water. "Just be prepared for a lot of texts from me, wondering what the hell is going on." Her laugh breaks through the yawn that's trying to escape, and then she says something to someone in the background. I assume it's Ben, her husband, who is everything a man should be...plus, he has a sexy accent.

"I wish I could be there for you tomorrow." I know she wants to be here. She's told me that a dozen times, but the girl runs around like crazy, trying to manage the store in the French Quarter. And Ben travels a lot, so I understand why she can't be here.

"Allie, you don't need to be here. I'm just being melodramatic. I'll be fine." It's true, tomorrow will be great, I'm just incredibly nervous. I'm used to being a worker, not the boss of a whole store, responsible for employees, schedules, and profits. I'm also nervous about the fact that the success of said store rests on skills I'm not even sure I have.

So...yes. Very nervous.

"You got that from me," she jokes, and I laugh. "I'll be down to see you by the end of the month. Hopefully, before the store opens, but I can't make any promises. Ben has a lecture in London at the end of the month, and I'm going with him, so it'll all depend on schedules." I sigh at the thought of getting on a plane and heading out of the country for a while. I left New York to get away from Aaron and the memories he ultimately ruined with his wandering dick, but being back here? At home? It's almost worse with a new set of memories assaulting me. I can't figure out which is the greater evil.

"Morgan? You there?" Her words shake me back to reality.

"Yeah, I'm here."

"You okay?" Am I? I know coming home was the right decision, and Allie offering me this job was a dream come true, but I'm starting to wonder if I should have started over somewhere else. Somewhere where no one knows my past or why I was forced to start over. Allie sighs, and I go and sit at my kitchen table that is currently covered in bubble wrap from all the plates my mother put away.

"Morgan, you don't have to do this, you know…" she says with such sincerity that I almost believe her.

"Yeah, right. If I back out now, you will be fucked."

"True." She sighs as I play with some hair that came loose from my ponytail. "But I would understand if you wanted to bail." As much as I dream of leaving and never coming back, that's not me. I need to face this. I need to face the future I've created for myself. Because the one I thought I would have disintegrated right in front of my eyes.

"I would never do that to you. Besides, being home isn't so bad. Home-cooked meals, I know where everything is, and you're my boss. What's so bad about that?"

"You sure?" she asks, and I smile, even though I know she can't see me.

"Yes, I'm sure. I want this store to be as successful as the first one." It's the truth. She's put so much effort into the original Hello Beautiful Boutique, I just don't want to let her down.

"It will be. You're the best in the business." I roll my eyes once again, and she scoffs as if she can see it. "You are. I don't want you thinking otherwise. I didn't give you this job because I feel sorry for you. I brought you on because you are an amazing person, you know fashion, and you ran your department at Bloomingdales like a drill sergeant. And that's what I need. I need a *me* in Miami, and you're the next best thing."

"Thanks."

I just hope I don't let her down.

3

OWEN

"It's about time you showed up," Matt calls as I close the door, locking it behind me. The guy looks as if he just rolled out of bed, his long, brown hair tied in a topknot as he struts around in his favorite grey sweatpants and a dirty t-shirt with our gym's name across the chest. I look at my watch and laugh.

"I'm only five minutes late, jackass." He throws a towel at me as I head behind the desk and turn on the computer. Matt and I opened this gym five years ago. We both graduated with majors in business and knew we wouldn't ever be a part of the corporate world. So, we took what we learned and applied it to something we both loved: fitness. Was it an overnight success? Hell, no. It took at least three years to get out of the red. But last year was our best year yet, with this year rivaling even those numbers.

"You know if you didn't own this place, I could fire you, right?" I give him the finger as I check my email, quickly making sure there are no cancelations for today's schedule.

Just as I'm about to log off, a new email pops up from one of my regulars. I open it and read:

Owen, sorry to do this to you last minute, but I have to cancel my session for this morning. Tommy was throwing up all night, and his fever has yet to go down, so I'm taking him to see the doctor. Sorry again. I'll still pay for the session, and I'll see you next week. —Amber

"Well, there goes my morning plans," I mutter to myself just as Matt comes over and leans against the desk.

"Amber cancel?" I nod, not surprised that Matt memorized my schedule. It's why I had no issues with going into business with him. He's organized, loyal, and has a memory that could rival Sheldon Cooper's. "You really gonna make her pay for the session?" he asks, giving me a look I know well.

"Of course, not. I'm not that big of an ass. Plus, her kid is sick. Ever since Ken left her, she's had a lot on her plate." When Amber started training with me, I knew she was motivated by her husband's infidelity, something she was very vocal about. I believe she said she wanted him to wish he never stuck his dick in another woman. I told her I would be happy to get her that revenge, even though she already looked amazing for a forty-year-old single mom.

"So, what are you gonna do now?" Matt asks, taking one of the mints from the bowl to my right and popping it into his mouth.

"I don't know. Might work out for a bit." He nods just as my phone goes off, A second later, it goes off again, then again. I sigh, knowing exactly who's blowing up my cell.

"You haven't cut her loose yet?" Matt asks with a knowing smirk that makes me feel like the biggest asshole on the planet. "Calm down, man. If it was me, I would probably keep her around, too. She must be one hell of a lay."

"Shut the fuck up and mind your own business," I grunt as he shrugs and goes back to cleaning the equipment. I pick up my mobile and see one missed call and four unread texts.

Bailey: *Morning, handsome, what are you up to today?*

Bailey: *Why aren't you answering my texts?*

Bailey: *Hello???*

Bailey: *Call me NOW.*

I sigh, pulling up her contact and pressing the phone to my ear. She picks up after the first ring.

"Where have you been?" she accuses as I tilt my head towards the ceiling, praying I can get through this conversation without blowing my top.

"Bails, you know I open the gym every day. I was busy talking to Matt about my schedule." She sighs, groaning into the phone, and for the millionth time this week, I wonder why I'm with her. In the beginning, it was amazing—she was hot, funny, and we had a great time together. Then, over time, she wanted more. More of my time, more of my attention, and more of my business. Bailey is an Instagram influencer and very proud of it. She should be, she's worked really hard to get where she is today, but it's become all-consuming. And she's using *my* brand, something that I built from the ground up, to gain more and more of a following for herself. And it's grating on my nerves.

It's become clearer as time goes on that she's with me for the clout and not for me, and I know I need to end it. For both of our sanities.

"You never have time for me anymore," she whines as I take a deep breath, needing strength to get through this conversation. There's a huge crash from the store next door, and I jump up from my seat.

"What was that?" Bailey asks as I motion to Matt that I'm going over to take a look. He nods as I head to the front door.

"Bails, I have to go. I'll talk to you later." I don't wait for her reply as I jerk open the front door and jog next door. The sign above the door says *Hello Beautiful Boutique,* and the door and windows are covered in brown paper, letting me know that it's under construction. I try the front door, and when it swings open, I walk inside.

"Hello? Is everyone okay?" I ask, hearing my voice echo through the small space. I don't see anyone around, but I do see a very large metal rack lying toppled on the floor and dust everywhere. The shop itself is pretty small, but from the looks of it, it's cute. The walls are plain white with paint chips taped to every available surface. The colors range from grey to bright pink and everything in between. I have no idea what this space will become, but right now, it's a mess.

"Hello! I just wanted to make sure no one's hurt after that thing fell," I call again, making my way farther into the space, stepping over the broken shelf and heading towards the back of the store.

"Sorry, yes, everything's fine. The stupid thing doesn't want to stay attached to the wall," a woman says from behind the counter. Her long, blond hair and curvy figure send a jolt through my body, but the minute she turns around, my whole world stops moving.

"Morgan?" I croak as I open my mouth to say something, anything…but nothing comes out. Morgan Lawson, the girl I spent most of my adolescence obsessing over is standing right in front of me. Given the color draining from her face, I would say she remembers exactly who I am, too. And from the fire I see in her eyes, she recalls precisely how much I ruined everything.

4

MORGAN

*T*his can't be happening right now. Who did I piss off in the universe for Owen Peters to be standing in front of me, looking like a tall drink of water, when I likely look like a hot mess? I mean, it's not fair that the man looks as if he could take off his shirt and be ready for a photo-shoot at *GQ*, and I probably look like the Crypt Keeper.

"What are you doing here, Owen?" I ignore the fact that he already told me he was making sure no one got hurt when the shelf fell, choosing instead to ask the question and hoping to get a different answer.

"I could ask you the same thing." His smirk sends unwanted heat down my spine, tingling the edges of my mind and conjuring up memories I wish I could forget. He stalks over to the shelving unit, picks it up as if it doesn't weigh a million pounds, and leans it against the wall. "The last I heard, you were some bigwig in New York City and were getting married." I swear I hear a growl at the last part of that sentence, but again, I choose to ignore it.

"Yeah, well, not everything you hear is the truth." His eyebrows rise in question, and I turn back around, hoping to make myself busy so he'll get the hint and leave so I can catch my breath.

"So, do you need any help getting this thing back up?" He indicates the shelf, and I inwardly groan at the fact that he didn't get the hint I so delicately placed in front of him, instead choosing to crowd my space, making it harder and harder for me to remember why I hate him so much.

Before I have a chance to tell him I have it covered, Becca comes in and smiles. I hired Becca once I knew this job was one hundred percent happening. Thank God, because she's saved me countless times over the past few weeks as I moved down the coast. She's quickly becoming my right-hand woman, and I love that I found her when I did.

"Well, hello there, handsome. What can I do for you?" Owen gives her his trademark smile that always got him whatever and whomever he wanted back in high school, and points to the rack.

"Just heard this thing fall, wanted to make sure everyone was okay." Becca practically sighs, and I swear I can see the heart emojis coming out of her eyes as she takes him in.

"Well, aren't you the sweetest thing I've ever seen?" Her Southern accent comes out stronger the longer they speak. If I didn't know better, I would think the heavy feeling growing in my stomach was jealousy, but that can't be right. Owen is nothing to me now.

"I was just asking Morgan if she needs any help putting it back on the wall. It looks like you need some anchors to make sure it doesn't fall again." I roll my eyes because, of course, he knows how to fix things. Add that to the list of traits I wish I didn't know; those that make him even hotter than he already is.

"That's so sweet of you!" Becca says, walking over to the wall and showing him where it needs to go.

"Okay, let me go to my truck. I'm pretty sure I have some anchors in my toolbox that we can use. If not, I'll just go to John's Hardware down the street and pick some up for you." Owen's eyes catch mine, as Becca continues talking about how sweet he is.

But I hear none of it. All I can concentrate on are his lips and the fact that I've fantasized about them for over ten years. And his eyes, that haven't left mine the entire time he's been talking to Becca. Once Owen leaves to get the supplies from his truck, Becca comes running over behind the counter and leans against the glass beside me.

"Holy. Shit. That boy is all muscle and good looks." She fans herself as if she's some damsel waiting for her prince charming, and I chuckle. Becca has been a source of entertainment since I arrived. And honestly, I know working with her is going to be a blast, but if she ends up getting her hands on Owen, I don't know how I'll react.

"Don't you think he's hot?" The question catches me off guard, and I drop the shoes I'm holding to the floor.

"Sure, if you like that kind of thing," I mutter, picking up the shoes and heading to the back room. Following me, Becca scoffs as if the idea of me not liking a tall, blond, muscled specimen is somehow against her religion. But the reality is, I *do* like that kind of thing. I *really* like that kind of thing. And right now, I'm reminding myself of the many reasons I *can't* like that kind of thing.

"You ladies want to show me exactly where this needs to go?" Owen calls from the front as he comes back in. Becca gives me a hopeful look, as if I'll give her permission to fawn over him, but I shake my head.

"You stay here and sort through these boxes. I need to know how much product we have before putting it out on the shelves." She frowns but nods her head, then picks up the box cutter next to her feet.

"Fine. But if it turns out that we're star-crossed lovers from another life, you're gonna be sorry!" I roll my eyes as I walk out of the back just as Owen bends over to get his tools off the floor.

Damn.

I forgot how good his ass looks. And in those basketball shorts? I can see everything.

"Morgan?" Owen calls, jerking me out of my daydream.

"Yes?" I say. My voice cracks, and from the small lift in his lips, he knows exactly what I was doing. I immediately want to dig myself a hole and jump into it.

"You wanna show me where this goes?" He points to the shelf that's still leaning against the wall. It really is a miracle that no one got hurt when it fell.

It's over six feet tall and could crush Becca or me easily.

"Yeah, sorry. It should go here..." I point to the spot where it was originally, hoping I don't have to find another place for it.

"Do you mind if we move it a bit to the left? I don't want to use the same holes since that part of the wall is a bit damaged and will only cause more issues later." I nod, not really trusting my voice. Owen pulls the shelf away from the wall, motioning for me to hold it upright as he marks the wall. It takes a beat, but after a minute, I can't stand the silence anymore.

"So, what are you up to now?" I groan at the awkwardness that seems to flow out of me whenever I'm around him. This never happened with Aaron. I was always so comfortable around him. But maybe that was the problem.

"I own the gym next door."

Of course, you do, I think as I watch him patch up the holes and take out a measuring tape from his toolbox.

"What do you mean, 'of course, you do?'" Fuck, I said that out loud? *Shit.*

"Um, I just meant that you were always into working out in high school, so it just doesn't surprise me that you own a fitness center." He gives me a look that lets me know that he doesn't believe a word that just came out of my mouth, but that he'll let it slide. Thank God.

"How long have you been home?" he asks, his eyes catching mine before going back to where he's drilling holes in the wall.

"A few days," I mutter, hoping he doesn't want more elaborate details of exactly *why* I came home.

"So, you're working here now?" he asks, and I can't help the small smile that creeps over my face when he's not looking, the butterflies flying fast and free inside my stomach.

"Yeah. A college friend needed someone to manage this place for her. She asked, and I said yes." It's the abridged version, but it's enough for now.

"So that rumor that you were getting married in New York, that was all a lie?" The pit reforms as my brain conjures up the image of Aaron and that woman in our kitchen. My eyes drift shut as I fight off the urge to punch something.

"Fuck. Sorry, M. I didn't mean to bring up bad shit." The use of my high school nickname makes me fight back the tears that are threatening to fall. "Hey," he whispers, the heat of his body washing over me the closer he gets. "You okay?" he asks softly, and I just nod my head, my eyes still closed.

"Yeah. I'm good." I open my eyes, briefly seeing the regret on his face before turning away and looking at the wall. "You okay to put this up? Or do you need me here?" I ask, hoping he doesn't need me around.

"I'm good. Although I wouldn't fight you if you want to stay." He winks, and I swear my entire body reacts, sending a shiver up my spine. Before I have a chance to utter an amazing sarcastic remark, he turns away and starts working again, leaving me to watch. And as much as I would love to stand here and ogle his backside, I make my way to the storage room, hoping to get the image of Owen's sad eyes, bright smile, and ridiculous body out of my mind before I do something stupid.

Like fall for him.

Again.

5

OWEN

*A*s I pull into the parking lot beside my gym, I can't help but gaze over to Hello Beautiful Boutique, wondering if Morgan's working. I spent the better part of last night trying to get her gorgeous face out of my head. Trying and failing to stop thinking about what her hair would feel like brushing against my bare chest, or how those full hips would feel under my fingers as I pull her closer until there isn't a single inch of space between us.

The first thought I had when I saw her again was that she looks even better than she did all those years ago. She had a rough go of it back then. And in the end, I probably made it worse. But I need to find a way to express how much I've regretted those decisions since the day she drove out of my life and never talked to me again.

"Owen! You coming in, or just sitting in your car and staring out the window all day?" Matt yells from the doorway as I shake myself out my memories and get out of the truck, heading toward the front door where he's waiting for me. I take one last look at Hello Beautiful Boutique before I follow Matt inside and lock the gym door behind us.

"Why are you here so early? You're always here right on time, except yesterday and I'm starting to think there's something wrong with you." Matt says nothing, just gives me the finger as he moves around the room and starts cleaning the machines one by one.

"What happened next door? Last I saw you, you were headed over there to see what happened." I smile to myself, remembering seeing Morgan for the first time and realizing that I had a second chance— not just to be her friend but to see if there could be something more.

"Yeah, turns out a shelf fell off the wall. I helped them put it back up and made sure it doesn't fall again." He gives me a look, and I roll my eyes. "What? That's exactly what happened."

"So, you're telling me a store selling shoes and shit is not run by a chick, and you just spent your day there yesterday because you're a nice guy and not because she's hot?" My mind goes in two different directions at once. Do I tell my best friend that the girl I was in love with in high school is now working next door, and I'm trying my hardest to get her to talk to me again? Or do I lie and tell him she's not hot, when in fact, she's the most beautiful woman I have ever laid eyes on?

"I was over there to help. That's it," I say, hoping he takes the hint and lets it go. Before he has a chance to come back at me with more smart-ass remarks, there's a banging on the front door. When I glance over my shoulder, I groan, seeing Bailey standing there, looking furious.

"What the fuck is your girlfriend doing here this early? Doesn't she have some kind of rule not to wake up before the sun?" I chuckle to myself as I throw a pencil at him as I head over to the door, opening it.

"Bails, what are you doing here? You know we don't open for another hour." She ignores me, brushing past me and entering the gym in a huff. I've learned over the last year that when Bails gets like this, I just need to let her be until she's ready to rant.

And I know a rant is coming; only I don't know what it'll be about today.

"How am I supposed to get exposure when brands won't give me a chance? I mean, that bitch Amy Welch gets every brand deal on the planet, and I can't even get one! I'm so much better than her. And have you seen her lately? I mean, skip a meal once in a while, you know?" Matt makes a sound, and Bails shoots him a look, to which he holds up his hands and walks to the back of the gym away from us, leaving me to fend for myself.

"Have you tried to look locally first? Maybe some of the places around here could use some exposure." It's an idea I've had for the gym, partnering with some other local businesses to see if it's mutually bencficial. I just need to run the idea by Matt first before I go knocking on doors.

"I already do that." I look at her questioningly, and she gives me that smile that I fell in love with when we first met. "That reminds me, I need you to shout me out today on your socials. I can do it for you if you want. I just need your passwords." I'm speechless. She's always used the success of my business for her personal gain, but it's never been this overt and out in the open. It puts a bad taste in my mouth.

"Who's that?" Bailey asks, pointing to the front door. When I see Morgan standing there in the early morning light, my chest compresses.

Fuck me, she looks gorgeous.

She's not wearing anything but yoga pants and a loose-fitting tank top, but for me, it's all she needs. A genuine smile crosses my face as I make my way to the door and open it, gesturing for her to come in. From the light gooseflesh on her arms, it's obvious the early morning air is a little nippy for her, so when she comes inside, and I shut the door, she breathes a sigh of relief.

"Damn, I forget how chilly the mornings can get here with the humidity," Morgan says, laughing to herself. She looks around the room, Matt coming up behind me with his hand extended.

"I'm Matt. Who might you be?" He's flirting, and every instinct in me screams to pull him aside and make it clear that she's off-limits. But then my eyes land on Bailey, who looks utterly pissed, and I feel like a complete jackass.

"I'm Morgan. I manage the shop next door. Or I will when we open." Recognition flashes across Matt's face as I shake my head, silently telling him that I'll explain everything later. But he ignores my pleading eyes.

"Next door? Please tell me you didn't have to watch this lug fix your shelves all day yesterday because that's just cruel."

Morgan's genuine laugh crests over the silence of the room as I breathe it in. "It wasn't so bad. Owen and I go way back, so..." She trails off, and I silently beg her to finish that sentence. But Matt interrupts again.

"You know Owen?" His eyes meet mine, the question in his gaze clear, but I shake my head slightly, not wanting Bails to get the wrong idea. Given the tension I can feel from where she's standing, the blowup is coming quicker than I want. "He never told me that, he just said he was helping the beautiful girl next door." I feel the rift immediately and brace myself.

Bailey makes an incredulous sound in the back of her throat as I stare at Matt, hoping he understands that I need him to get Morgan as far away from Bailey as possible. When he nods slightly, taking Morgan's hand and leading her across the room, I sigh in relief.

"You know her?" Bailey asks, venom dripping from her tone as my eyes reluctantly leave Morgan and focus on the woman in front of me.

"We grew up together. Went to the same high

school." Relegating Morgan to just an old acquaintance seems wrong, especially when our relationship means so much on so many levels.

"You know, if you were really her friend, you'd get her on that treadmill and on a meal plan. Because, honey, she's going to be bad for business." The giggle that escapes her puts a sour taste in my mouth, and it grows the longer I stare at Bailey, wondering who this woman is and why I didn't see it before. Every word out of her mouth disgusts me, and yet my first instinct is to check on Morgan, make sure she didn't hear the vile words that just came out of Bailey's mouth. When I glance over and see that she's still engrossed in a conversation with Matt, I take a deep breath. *Thank God.*

"Bails, I think it's time you go. I've got a client coming in." Bailey eyes me, then her gaze drifts over to Morgan, who is now looking right at us. The sinking feeling permeates the pit of my stomach, and before I have a chance to walk away, Bailey grabs the back of my neck and seals her lips to mine. I try and pull away as gracefully as I can, but it's no use. The moment she moans into my mouth, I know exactly what she's doing, and the anger builds the longer her arms are around my neck. Just as I'm about to pull her off me, Bailey moves back, smiling up at me as she leans in and kisses the tip of my nose lightly as if we're in a fucking sitcom.

"You know you should ask her to join." She points directly at Morgan. "Big girls usually travel in packs. It'd be great for business." I'm about to say something when she kisses my cheek and saunters out of the gym as if she didn't just say something incredibly demeaning and utterly disgusting.

The silence is deafening as the front door closes. When I turn to Morgan, the sadness that permeates those gorgeous eyes of hers rips me in half. When I open my mouth to try and say something—anything —to erase what just happened, she stops me.

"I'll see you later," she says quietly as she turns to Matt. "It was nice to meet you, Matt." He gives her a small smile as we both watch her walk out the door.

6

MORGAN

"You seem tense," Kennedy states as I make my way into her office and flop down on her couch. I take the pillow that sits beside me and fold it over my stomach, hugging it close.

"You know, for a therapist, you're very observant." My tone drips with sarcasm as the events of the last few days wash over me, and I fight tooth and nail to stop the tears that have been burning behind my eyelids for the past twenty-four hours. Kennedy eyes me as I sit , stewing in my stubbornness. And I know from experience that she won't say anything until I do. So, we remain silent for what feels like an hour but can only be five minutes before I crack. "Yes, I'm tense. It's been a rough week."

"What happened?" Kennedy leans back in her chair, her notepad balancing on her knees as she waits for me to spill my guts. I've been in therapy for years, longer than I've had a full-time job. And, honestly, it's a savior. But Kennedy and I have only known each other for as long as I've been in Miami, so our relationship isn't what I need it to be right now. There's nothing I can do about that, however.

"I ran into someone from my past." I'm knowingly being vague, and from the arched brow Kennedy angles my way, I know she sees right through me. "You want me to say their name." It's not a question, only because I know in my gut that's what her silence means. After another minute of her stare down, I cave. "Fine. I ran into Owen."

"And who is Owen to you?" she asks, writing some notes on her pad of paper, her eyes never leaving mine.

"He was my high school best friend."

"Was?" Her question catches me off guard. I don't know why, because using the past tense when referring to Owen isn't anything new. He hasn't been a part of my life for a very long time. But for some reason, right now, the realization that he isn't my best friend anymore hits me harder than I imagined.

"Did something happen between the two of you for you not to speak for over ten years?"

Flashes of prom come flying back, the amazing dress I picked out, the idea of Owen and me going together, and me finally telling him how I felt. Then I remember everything crashing down when he didn't show up and ignored me until all I felt was alone and heartbroken.

When I tell Kennedy about that night, she says nothing, just writes something on the pad in front of her. When her eyes meet mine again, I don't see the pity I usually see when I tell that story, and that throws me.

"So, what happened after that?" she asks, and I sit there dumbfounded. She just bypassed one of the hardest moments of my life as if it were a feather falling from the sky. Just waved it away without a care in the world. That moment defined my next five years, creating a systematic response to anyone who tried to get close. The only exception to that rule was Allie, and that's only because she weaseled her way in and didn't give me the chance to say no. And I'm thankful for her every day.

"What happened was, I moved away to go to school and never spoke to him again."

"Until yesterday," she states matter-of-factly. I

hug the pillow tighter as I nod my head, not really having the ability to speak. "So, what did seeing him do to you?" I want to be mad at her for making me rehash this, but that's why I came here, after all. I know if I don't talk about it, everything will get bottled up, and that low-hanging cloud will start to follow me wherever I go.

"At first, I was surprised. Then I was pissed, then when we started talking I…" I trail off, not knowing if I want to admit the growing feelings that still stir inside me.

"You started to feel something for him again," she answers for me as I nod silently, feeling the tears start to fall as the weight of what those feelings mean for the fragile walls I've tried to build since I left Aaron settles. Kennedy places her notepad on the floor beside her as she leans forward, her hands folded neatly in her lap. "Are those tears because you're scared of Owen or something else?"

It's a leading question, and I almost laugh at how good she is at making me spill my guts. She's worth every penny I pay her.

"Owen doesn't scare me. I think I'm just cautious of him." Kennedy stares, giving me a look that says she knows there's more to it than that. "Well, you know my weight has always been an underlying issue for me. And ever since I left Aaron, I've been trying to get that under control. Attempting to love myself for the woman I am in this body, instead of waiting to love myself in the body that everyone else will love." She gives me a small smile and nods her head for me to continue. "I guess I'm just worried that he sees me the same way Aaron did."

"And what way is that?" Ugh. She's going to make me say it.

"Fat. I'm worried he sees me as the fat girl I still see in the mirror every morning. And since he's so...fit, I'm worried he'll look at me like a pet project." Kennedy picks up her notepad once more and sits back in the chair, her legs crossing in front of her.

"Morgan, you need to understand that you can't place your weight issues on others. Aaron might have used it against you, but you can't let one person's opinion cloud your judgement of others. That is exactly what others have done to you."

Damn, she's right.

THERE'S nothing like going from a therapy session to work in the span of a few hours. And even worse? As

47

I walk up to the front door, Owen is there, leaning against the side of my building, waiting for me. *Fuck.* He looks gorgeous with that backwards baseball hat covering his blond hair. The blue fabric makes his eyes pop. As my hand reaches for the front door's handle, his shadow overtakes me, and I feel the heat of his chest against my back.

"What do you want, Owen?" I know I told Kennedy that I was going to give him a chance to redeem himself, but the moment I see that sweet smile and dimple on his right cheek, I can't help the anger that surges through my body. That face was the star of every fantasy I had as a teen. And now when I see him, all I remember are the tears streaming down my face as my mom comforted me in the living room, and my dad threatened to kill Owen.

"I just wanted to come by and apologize for Bailey. She was out of line yesterday." A scoff of disbelief escapes me as I turn, making Owen back up just an inch.

"Out of line?" His eyes plead with mine to understand where he's coming from, but I'm not willing to give his *girlfriend* a pass because he's *sorry* she said something she clearly meant to say. "Owen, you don't need to apologize for something your girlfriend said. It's not your fault." The more his eyes bore into mine, the more the anger begins to dissipate, and those feelings that Kennedy tried to uncover start to rear their ugly head.

"You have to know that what she said isn't true, right?" The words sink into my skin as I start to process the idea of Owen not thinking that I'm overweight.

"Come on, Owen. I've spent my entire life dodging the looks, the whispers and crude gestures. I'm just not used to the comments being hurled at my face." He flinches, and I know I need to leave—for both our sakes.

"M, please. Just talk to me." His eyes plead with me as I ignore the pull I feel toward him and turn and open the door to the shop.

"I have to get to work. I'll see you around." With that, I head inside. The moment the door shuts behind me, I lean against it, close my eyes, and wonder how the hell I'm going to get through being around Owen Peters for the foreseeable future.

7

OWEN

I can't stop pacing. The way Morgan walked away from me earlier haunts me, to the point where I've been forcibly keeping myself from going over there and ruining the rest of her night by talking to her about the disgusting things that Bails said. That sad, broken look that crossed Morgan's eyes when Bailey mentioned her weight left a sinking hole inside me. Because I've never seen anything but the beautiful girl she refuses to see.

I wish I had her phone number. At least I could text her, make sure she's okay. But I know she'd likely hate that. I could always go see her parents since I know they never moved from Morgan's childhood home. But they haven't been that welcoming to me since prom night—and what happened. Even though I tried to explain why I did what I did, they refused to hear it. They told me that I needed to tell the one person who deserved an explanation. Unfortunately, by that time, Morgan had moved thousands of miles away, and I was left with a lifetime of regret.

So, I continue to pace until I hear a knock at my front door. For a split second, I wonder if the fates are being kind to me today. Maybe it's Morgan standing beyond that threshold, waiting for me to explain everything. But when I open it, it's Bailey, arms crossed, looking as if she hates my guts.

"I can't believe you!" She storms past me, leaving me to hold the door open as my eyes track her movements throughout my house. First, she makes her way into my kitchen, takes out a bottle of water from my fridge, and then heads to my cupboard and grabs a protein bar she knows I always have on hand. Usually, the thought of Bailey making herself at home makes me feel like our relationship has some kind of normalcy to it. But lately when she's here, all I can think about is getting her to leave so I can have some time to myself.

"What are you talking about?" She can't mean what happened with Morgan. That would be insane.

"You couldn't keep your eyes off her! I was

standing right there and all you were doing was looking at her! I'm your girlfriend, not her." I guess she *is* insane because no scenario on this Earth would allow me to side with someone who treats people the way Bailey did with Morgan yesterday. I've created a business around helping both men and women be confident however they see fit. It could be losing weight, gaining muscle, or just learning how to be healthy in their everyday life. Bailey telling me that I should have taken her side when she was insulting someone I care about makes me question not only her morals but also what I saw in her in the first place.

"Bails, we need to talk." From the way the bottle of water stalls on the way to her lips, and her wide eyes plead with mine, she knows what's coming. All the fight from a second ago leaves her, and her body language changes in front of me. She stands up straighter, her eyes narrow, and she takes deliberate steps toward me. This conversation has been a long time coming. I had this thought in my head way before Morgan showed up, but now, the idea of being with someone when I know my heart belongs to the girl that got away doesn't seem fair.

"Don't you dare say what you're about to, Owen," she demands, her voice stern as she sets everything in her hands down on the table in front of her and places her fists on her hips. "You will not break up with me when you know we're meant to be together." There's a slight hint of panic in her tone, and I know she's not worried about not being with me. She's concerned about her access to my gym. I take a deep breath and sit down on the couch.

"Bails, you know this hasn't been working for a long time," I start, but she comes over and straddles me, sitting on my lap, her breasts directly in front of my face. As a guy, I notice how amazing they look in the loose-fitting top that hangs off one shoulder. But the reality is, the woman in front of me doesn't have the same appeal she did all those months ago.

"Owen, baby." She moans as she hooks her arms around my neck, pulling me closer so she can take my earlobe into her mouth and lightly tease my flesh. Her hips circle over my cock, hoping to garner some kind of reaction like she used to, but I feel nothing. I wish I loved her the way I thought I did back when we started dating. But in reality, everything has been slowly falling apart around me, and it took Morgan coming home to put things into perspective.

"Bails, stop." I pull away from her eager lips. When I see the dramatic pout on her face, I know

I'm making the right decision. That the only thing I want to do is roll my eyes when I see that look should tell me everything I need to know.

"Owen, come on. You can't seriously be thinking of ending things. We're so amazing together." This time, I *do* roll my eyes as I pick her up and place her on the couch beside me.

"We haven't been together for months, and you know that." She starts to shake her head, fingers inching closer and closer to my knees. I get up and start pacing the living room again.

"What is this really about?" She stands, hands on her hips again, waiting for my response. And, truth be told, I don't know if I have a definitive answer for her. I know she wants me to say Morgan's name, but I won't do it under any circumstances. I know the minute her name leaves my mouth, Bailey will make sure to cause as much damage as possible, and I refuse to bring that down on Morgan.

"What do you want me to say, Bailey? I just can't see this working, and I think it's better if we stop seeing each other." Argh, even hearing the words makes me want to cringe. I sound like every bad romance movie in the world. The difference here is that I mean every word, no matter how clichéd it sounds.

"You're so pathetic, Owen." I take another deep breath, closing my eyes and counting to ten before I try explaining things one more time. But before I have the chance, Bailey continues her rant. "I can't believe you are choosing to dump...this." She motions to her body as if it's the eighth wonder of the world. "For what?" Her eyes search mine, and I try my hardest not to give her any nuggets of info that she can use against me. "Please tell me this has nothing to do with that girl from yesterday." Her inflection bleeds disgust as I let out a groan that surprises us both.

"Bails, this is about you and me. It has nothing to do with anyone else. I promise." But I can tell she doesn't believe me, because before I can explain myself again, she storms toward the front door.

"You'll regret this, Owen. Soon, you'll realize that we're meant to be together. That's *my* promise." And with that, she opens the door and then slams it behind her, leaving me to take the first deep breath I've taken in months.

IT DOESN'T TAKE LONG to get to the beach, but when I park my truck and open the door, the scent of saltwater and fresh air hits me, and I instantly calm down. I've been coming here since I was a teenager, and no matter what day of the week or time of day or season, it always calms my nerves and allows me to see things a little more clearly.

I head toward my favorite spot, one that I found my junior year. It's hidden under an old pier. Over the years, I've created a pretty neat space. Old tree stumps act as stools, and to the naked eye, it seems like an abandoned spot. But to me, it's my salvation. What I don't expect to see when I approach is a figure sitting on my favorite stump, looking out at the water, bundled in a bright blue sweatshirt and neon pink leggings. I know only one person who loves that color combo, and my heart starts to race as I make my way toward her.

"Morgan?" I whisper, hoping I don't scare her. But from the way she jumps off the stump and almost falls on her ass, I know I didn't do a good job.

"Owen? What are you doing here?" she asks, wide-eyed and so fucking beautiful. She has no makeup on, and her hair is up in a crazy bun on the top of her head. Although I can see the apprehension in her gaze, those eyes slay me.

"I was going to ask you the same thing." She gives me a shy smile as she turns to look back at the water.

"I didn't think you'd remember this place," I say, picking up one of the stumps and setting it beside her. Once I sit down, my eyes catch the side of her face, and for the first time in years, I feel a weight lift off my chest. She's here. She's back in my life. And although I know a part of her still hates me, I don't care right now. As long as she's here, I know I have a chance to change her mind.

"This spot saved me on more than one occasion when we were in high school. I remember I came here the day after prom." Her voice cracks, and as much as I don't want to get into it, I know it's time we talked about what happened.

"I know you hate me for that night," I start, watching a shuddering breath leave Morgan's body. If it weren't for the way her fingers play with the fabric of her leggings, I'd think she wasn't listening. "I never meant for you to hate me." She scoffs but still doesn't look toward me. So, I continue. "I tried to find you for years, but your parents are like a vault. They wouldn't tell me where you went at first." That gets her attention, and when her eyes focus on mine, my heart breaks at the tears threatening to fall.

"You tried to find me?" I nod as she turns toward me fully. "Why?" Her question catches me off guard.

Because her not realizing the impact she's had on my life is something I need to rectify.

"M, you were the most important thing in my life. And then, all of a sudden, you were gone, and I couldn't find you, and I didn't know what to do…" A barking laugh escapes as Morgan gets up and starts walking away. Before I have a chance to follow, she stops and turns, clearly pissed.

"I was the most important thing in your life? Come on, Owen. You didn't give two shits about me. That was crystal-clear when you left me to wait hours for you on prom night and then ignored every text I sent for the next two days!" My heart breaks as her tears fall, and I have to fight every instinct in me not to grab her and wrap her in my arms. Because I know that will only make this whole thing worse.

"I wanted to bring you that night, okay! I wanted more than anything to take you to that dance and watch you smile as we both danced horribly. I wanted to see you in your dress because I know you would have looked so beautiful. But most of all, I wanted to go with you because the idea of *not* going with you made my heart break." Everything around us stops, and for a split second, I wonder if I said too much.

"What are you talking about? You stood me up!"

She flings her arms to the sides, and I stand, slowly walking toward her.

"I had to! If I didn't, they would've made your life a living hell!" Her eyes shoot to mine, uncertainty reflecting back at me.

"What are you talking about?" I can't help my fingers from pulling at the edges of my hair as I try to find the words to explain the shit show that was our senior year.

I sit back down on the stump, my head in my hands as I start to explain as best I can. "It was supposed to be the night I finally... It was supposed to be the best night of my life. But then Kelly found out and ruined everything..." I mutter. I can't even tell if she's listening, and I stare at the sand, my emotions overwhelming. When I feel her kneel in front of me, I look up, meeting her beautiful eyes.

"Found out about what?" she whispers as if she's afraid to hear the answer, but I see the determination in her gaze. I know this is it. This is the moment that could change everything.

"She found out that I was in love with you."

8

MORGAN

*M*y alarm sounds, and I groan, turning to shut the damn thing off. I had the worst night's sleep, and I know it's because I spent most of the night replaying what Owen said and trying to figure out what to do next.

Don't get me wrong, hearing someone tell you they were in love with you is extremely flattering, but when it's your ex-best friend who you now hate but were also in love with for most of your childhood, it makes things a little more complicated. I mean, does he *still* love me? I shake my head. Of course, not. He has a girlfriend—a very beautiful one at that—and him leaving her to be with me is laughable.

After he dropped that bombshell of a statement, I

don't remember anything but laughing to myself as I walked away. He tried to get me to stay and talk, but I was beyond talking at that point. I couldn't picture the captain of the football team, the most popular guy in school, being in love with the chubby girl who lived down the street. To me, it just wasn't plausible. So, I walked away.

I regret it now, thinking about every word, every look, and every gesture he made last night. *Why didn't I stay? Ask how? Why? Find out what changed?* But the idea of bringing it up now after I walked away the way I did makes me sick to my stomach. I guess I'll just have to ignore him for the rest of my life...right?

I head into the shower, making sure to blast music so I don't stand there and overthink every part of that conversation. When I'm done, I get ready as quickly as possible because the grand opening of Hello Beautiful Boutique is in a few days, and I know there is a ton of stuff to do—and thinking about Owen is not one of them. I pick my phone up off the bed and see a text from Allie.

Allie: *How's my store doing? Are you excited about opening next week?*

I text back that everything is going smoothly,

that the store looks awesome, and that everything is set for the grand opening.

Allie: *I knew I picked the right girl for the job!*

I know she's one of my closest friends but hearing that from her makes me extremely proud. I just hope that she likes what I've done with the store when she comes down next week.

Me: *When does your flight come in again? I wanna meet you at the airport!*

It doesn't take long for her to respond, and I make sure to write down the date and time so I don't forget. Because knowing me, if I don't set a reminder, I will definitely be getting a text from Allie telling me that she's landed, and I'm nowhere near the airport. I put my phone into my purse and make my way to the store.

When I get there, Becca is standing outside, talking to Owen. I don't know why I feel the surge of jealousy I do the moment I see them, but I push it down, calling Becca to the front door.

"Morning, M," Owen calls from next door, and I give him a curt nod, saying nothing as I open the store and let myself in. I know I'm purposefully ignoring him, but I'm not ready to talk about what happened. And from the look on his gorgeous face, that's all he wants to do.

"Wow, you're in a bad mood today," Becca groans as I sigh, knowing I am, and I don't ever want to take my bad moods out on her.

"Sorry. I had a rough night." She nods as we set our stuff down behind the front counter, and I turn and survey what we have to do today.

"I might have something to pick your day up!" Becca says, clapping beside me. From the excited look on her face, I know immediately that I will not enjoy whatever she has in store for me.

"Please tell me you didn't do anything to the store..." The dread creeps up because Allie and I have talked at length about what the aesthetic of this place should be and worked endless hours designing every last detail and making sure it's exactly what she wants.

"Of course, not!" she says, smiling. I pull out my to-do list and begin walking around the store, making new line items as I go so I don't forget. "But I did set you up on a blind date tonight." I stop dead in my tracks. She didn't say what I think she said...did she?

I slowly turn, only to see the face-splitting smile on Becca's face. She looks so proud of herself, so happy that she did this for me. I try to ignore the gut-wrenching, sinking feeling trying to overtake my body.

"What?" I choke out, hoping to God I heard her wrong.

"Yeah! This guy I know from the coffee shop asked me out. I turned him down but said I had a hot friend that he should go out with. And he said yes! Isn't that amazing?" Everything she just said makes me break out in hives. Knowing that he asked her out first makes me wonder what he's going to think of me. Becca is gorgeous with her long, wavy, chestnut hair, tanned skin, and hazel eyes. To compare the two of us would be lunacy. Second, she called me *hot*, something no one has ever said when describing me before, so that's a red herring if I ever heard one. Nothing about this sounds *amazing*.

"Um, I don't think I'm ready to date yet," I mumble, avoiding her eyes and scanning the room one more time before making my way to the back to get some more products to display.

"Come on, Morgan! I know you just got out of a long relationship, but you need to get back out there! What's the worst that can happen?" As a person who constantly worries about almost everything, that is the last thing she should have said to me. I give her a look that lets her know I have a list in my brain of things that could go horribly wrong, but she just waves me off and comes over to where I'm standing. "This could be a good thing. Get yourself out there again...get laid." As much as I want to scold her for being so interested in my sex life, she's not wrong. It's been a long time since a man was anywhere near my body, and as much as I try to fight it, I crave it.

"Fine," I relent, knowing this could end in disaster. "I'll go. But if this turns out to be a nightmare, you are working nights for the rest of the month." Becca winks as she tells me all the details I need to know to meet the guy tonight.

God help me.

I KNEW I should have stayed home. I also knew that going on a blind date was the worst idea ever, but I didn't listen to my gut. I listened to Becca because she dangled the idea of sex in my face. We are miles away from that scenario, and all I want to do is crawl under the table and hide for the foreseeable future.

Marshall sits in front of me, giving the waitress eyes as she flirts with him directly in front of me. He's good-looking in a classic way—dark hair, light eyes, and a jaw that could cut glass. When I walked up, I hoped this might go well...that notion died quickly.

Now, I'm holding up my menu, hoping this date ends sooner rather than later. At first, I thought it was going okay. He pulled out my chair when I sat down, asked me about my job, and how it was moving from New York to Miami. Everything seemed great until we ordered food. The second I opened my mouth, he stopped me. Instead, he turned to the waitress and said, "She'll have the avocado salad, dressing on the side...obviously." They both snickered as he ordered a steak with a side of potatoes, the one thing on this awful menu I wanted to order. When I told him that I didn't like avocado, he just shrugged and said, "It's good for you, you should try it," before handing both menus to the waitress.

I let that one slide because I thought it was just a one-off, but the longer we sit, the more uncomfortable I become. He watches as I eat the disgusting salad, commenting on how leaving the vegetables to the side—something I've done since I was a kid— negates the healthy choice of the salad. I want to tell him that maybe *he* should eat them since he ordered for me, but I keep my mouth shut.

When I ask the waiter for a slice of cheesecake,

and Marshall says, "We're not having dessert, thanks," I decide that's it.

"You know what, Marshall? I'm done. I would say it was nice to meet you, but that would be a lie. And since you haven't held your tongue all night regarding my weight, I'm not going to stay quiet either." His eyes narrow as I stand, smoothing out my little black dress, ready to bolt the second I'm done talking. "You might be good-looking, but that is the only good thing about you. You are crass, cocky, and so unbelievably self-involved that being in a conversation with you is a nightmare. I hope we never meet again." I give him a small wave right before I grab my purse from the back of the chair and head outside.

The cool breeze sends a chill up my spine as I try and hail a cab. Unfortunately, I come up empty, so I start walking. After a few minutes, I curse the high heels I chose to wear tonight, feeling their bite and knowing that if I don't stop walking soon, I'll regret it later.

As I stop in front of an old ice cream shop to give my feet a break, I can't help but stare at my reflection. When I left my house earlier, I figured I looked good. I thought the dress showed off my best curves, and the heels showcased how long my legs can appear when I try hard enough. But the longer I stand here staring, the more I notice my imperfections. The way my love handles pop out, even though I wore Spanx for that specific reason. The way my arm fat settles against me when my arms dangle at my sides. Even the double chin that I thought I had grown accustomed to over the years seems to mock me, reminding me of every word Marshall said.

I finally hail a cab at the corner and tell the driver to take me to Hello Beautiful Boutique right before the tears start to fall. I know I should probably go home, but the idea of being there, alone, with just my thoughts, sends me into an anxious spiral.

Keeping myself busy sounds like a brilliant idea.

9

OWEN

"You staying late?" Matt asks as he picks up his bag and heads for the front door. I've been here all day, and I'm exhausted. But the idea of going home doesn't appeal either. I've spent most of the day looking out the window, hoping to catch a glimpse of Morgan as she leaves, but I must have missed her because Becca left hours ago, and the lights have been out ever since.

"Yeah, I have a few things left to do," I lie, hoping he buys it and leaves. His expression tells me he doesn't, but he leaves anyway. I spend the next few minutes browsing the internet on my phone until I see headlights. When I look outside, a cab pulls up and stops in front of Hello Beautiful Boutique.

Before I have a chance to guess who's in the car, the door opens, and Morgan steps out. At first, I almost don't recognize her because she has makeup on, her hair is down, and she's wearing a little black dress that hugs her curves in a way that makes my cock rock-hard. She looks absolutely gorgeous.

But the minute I see her face, everything changes. The tear stains that streak down her cheeks, the puffiness around her eyes, and the sadness that radiates off her entire body makes me jump from where I stand and open the front door.

"Morgan? Are you okay?" She startles, holding a hand to her chest.

"Fucking hell, you scared the crap out of me." She wipes away a stray tear from her cheek as I make my way over to her. "I didn't think you'd be here this late," she murmurs as I get closer and fight the urge to pull her to me.

"What happened?" My voice is calm, but in reality, all I want to do is rip open whoever made her feel this way.

"It's nothing. It's not important." Fuck that.

"Don't tell me that seeing you get out of a cab at your place of business, crying, looking like you just came back from a date isn't important. What happened?" Her shoulders fall, her chin dropping to her chest as her whole body starts to shake. It takes me all of three seconds to realize that she's crying, and I lose the fight. I wrap my arms around her and bring her against my chest.

Fuck, it feels amazing to have her against me.

"Baby, please. Tell me what happened." She stiffens in my hold. Then, all of a sudden, she pushes me away. I stagger back. "Morgan?"

"You do not get to call me *baby*. Not after everything," she croaks, and my heart sinks a little. I knew telling her that I loved her was a long shot, but I didn't expect her to hate me even more than she did before.

The tears start to fall once more, and when I take a step toward her again, she backs away. So, I hold my hand up and retreat a small step.

"M, I just want to make sure you're okay, that's all." She shakes her head and turns around, heading for the shop's front door. "Please, just tell me. Did someone hurt you?" My mind is going to the darkest places at this point. I want her to tell me that I don't need to go and kill someone tonight.

"Hurt me?" she says with a scornful laugh. "You mean like when you're on a blind date, and that person uses the entire dinner to comment on how fat you are? Or when you didn't want to go on said date at all because you knew you weren't ready, yet do it anyway and hope for the best, only to be scolded for wanting dessert?" What the actual fuck? Who was this guy?

"Morgan, you know that's not true, right? That guy's an asshole." She starts shaking her head, and this time the tears cut me so deeply that I refuse to stay where I am. I wrap my arms around her once more. Thankfully, she comes willingly.

"It is true…" she mumbles into my shirt, but instead of making her explain, I pull her closer, basking in the feel of her in my arms.

"Morgan. You are not fat, and anyone who tells you differently doesn't know what's in front of them." I know she doesn't believe me, and I know from experience that it takes more than one or two nice comments to make someone realize that the person they see in the mirror isn't the one everyone else sees.

"What if you helped?" Her voice is small, and I barely hear her as her breath cascades over my skin. It takes everything in me not to fantasize about what those lips would feel like skimming the side of my neck. "What if you trained me…?" The hopeful tone of her voice leads me to believe that she thinks I'll be able to change everything she hates about herself, when in reality, I do the opposite. I try to get my clients to accept the person on the outside and begin to love the person on the inside. But right now, I know that's not what she wants to hear.

"You want me to train you?" I clarify as she steps away, her eyes pleading with me to accept. "Are you sure that's what you want? I don't want you to change yourself because someone else told you to. That's not how this works." I really want to say that no matter what she thinks of herself, nothing she does will ever change the way I feel about her. But I don't. I know that what I said to her yesterday freaked her out, and I saw the look she gave me as she walked away and again this morning when she ignored me.

"Owen, I know you're all about making women feel good about themselves. And that's great. But right now, you need to see the desperate woman begging for your help. I know I need to love myself, but right now, I can't see past the hateful comments Marshall hurled at me tonight. I need you to help me. Please." Fuck, I can't say no to that. It's impossible.

"Fine," I relent. The smile that crosses her face takes away all the doubt I processed. Because right now? Right now, she looks like the girl I fell in love with all those years ago, the one that loved puzzles, hated pineapple on pizza, and wanted nothing more than to be a fashion designer. "But I want you to understand something. Just because I agree to train you doesn't mean I'm going to be any different to you than I am to my other clients. That means you will follow my every instruction. You will trust my judgment. And the most important one of all, you will be patient."

Her eyes narrow in confusion. "Be patient? What does that have to do with anything?" she asks as I give her a small smile.

"I need you to be patient because there will come a time in the next few weeks where you'll be discouraged, and I need you to remember that this is a marathon not a race." She rolls her eyes at the cliché, and I chuckle because most of my clients hate that saying. But the reason I use it is because it's true.

"That is the worst way to motivate someone," she says, smiling. For a second, I just bask in it. "So, what you're telling me is that I need to trust you?" I nod. "Then, fine. But I reserve the right to have one meltdown a month, okay?" I laugh because if I get to spend the next few months this close to her, I'll take whatever she can give me.

"Are you sure you want this? It won't be easy," I

admit, but she just nods her head and leans in, kissing me on the cheek.

My heart stops when her lips meet my skin, and from the way her body locks in place, I think she feels it, too.

"Let me drive you home," I say, not wanting her to be alone out here in the dark. When she nods, I lock up the shop and lead her to my truck. Once inside, we fall into silence as I drive her home, only speaking when she tells me where to turn. All too soon, we arrive at her place, and I turn to look at her.

"You work tomorrow?" I ask. She nods her head. "Do you want to start training then?"

"Sure, but I close tomorrow so I won't be done until after eight." I give her a small smile and place my hand on hers, feeling the warmth of her skin against mine as it sends waves of desire coursing through me. I know if I don't let her go right now, I will spill my guts and freak her out.

"Doesn't bother me. Come to the gym after you're done. I'll be waiting." She smiles, then opens her door and gets out. Before she walks up her driveway, she turns and looks back at me.

"Thank you, Owen, I really appreciate it." I give her one last smile as she heads up to her door and goes inside. I wait for her to look back, but she doesn't. My feelings may be one-sided right now, but I *have* to try and win her over. When she's safely in the house, I lean back and smile. Tonight showed me a lot of things. But most importantly, it revealed that baby steps are the way to show Morgan the amazing woman she is—the gorgeous female I see.

And when the day finally comes, and she realizes exactly that, I vow to make her feel that way for the rest of her life.

10

MORGAN

I've been dreading this all day. As much as I want to lose weight, the idea of working out has always scared the crap out of me. The thought of running, jumping, or even stretching in public is utterly terrifying. But add Owen to that, watching me? It's possibly my worst nightmare.

I take a deep breath, grab the duffle bag I brought to work with me this morning, and head toward the front door. I do one last sweep, making sure that all the lights are off, and as I take in the store, I can't help but smile. The place looks amazing. Racks of clothing, hats on every shelf, and shoes everywhere. It's a girly-girl's dream, and I hope Allie approves when she comes into town in a few days.

The moment I shut the door and lock it behind

me, I hear a throat clear. I look to my right as Owen leans against the brick wall that separates our buildings.

"You ready?" he asks as I take in his backwards ball cap, oversized white t-shirt, and basketball shorts. The more I'm around Owen, the more I realize that he doesn't wear much else. But to be honest, I'm not complaining.

"As I'll ever be," I mumble, making my way to him and feeling the butterflies in my stomach take flight. Owen must notice my apprehension because before he opens the door to the gym, he stops me, grips both of my shoulders in his hands, and then leans down so his eyes are level with mine.

"I want you to know that there is no judgement when you walk through that door. I will never think less of you if you can't do something, I will never comment on your weight—good or bad—because that's not why we're here. I am here to help you get to where *you* want to be, not where I think you should be. Okay?" I nod my head, but my hands start to shake nonetheless. "Morgan. You have nothing to be ashamed of or scared of, okay? If it makes you feel better, we can always meet at night when no one is in the gym. Whatever makes you the most comfortable." God, he's being so sweet. And the longer I stare into his eyes, the more I want to believe that the feelings he had for me back in high school aren't gone. That he still feels that way. But then I remember that he has a girlfriend, and I push all those things aside.

"What about Bailey?" I ask. His head tilts to one side as if he's questioning why I would bring her up. "Won't she be upset that you're spending all this time with me after you close?" He gives me a huge smile, something I did not expect.

"I'm not with Bailey anymore," he says casually as he opens the gym door and motions for me to enter in front of him. But I don't. I just stand there, dumbfounded that he just blurted that out as if it doesn't change everything.

"What? What do you mean you're not with Bailey anymore?" He shakes his head, placing a hand on the small of my back as he pushes me through the door.

"It means…I'm not with Bailey anymore," he states matter-of-factly, shutting the door behind us and locking it, making sure no strays come in after hours. "You should go get changed. The locker rooms are back there." He points to a hallway to my left, and I give him a curt nod. If he doesn't want to elaborate, then I won't ask—even though that's all I want to do.

I head into the locker room, change into new yoga pants—since that seems to be my daily wardrobe right now—and a sports bra. I walk out of the changing space and face the mirror, and my heart sinks. The extra skin on my arms, the bulging area between my sports bra and high-waisted pants. These are all things I notice every day and seem to ignore, but right now? In this fluorescent lighting, they are all I can see. I head back to my bag, grab a loose-fitting t-shirt, and throw it on.

"You okay in there?" Owen yells from down the hall. I yell back that I'm fine, but when I make my way back to where he's waiting for me, I realize that I'm not. And I won't be if he continues standing there looking like a tall drink of water. The man shed his shirt, and his spectacular abs are on full display. My eyes have no choice but to soak in every inch of his tanned skin, his sculpted chest, and those sexy v-shaped muscles that lead the eyes straight to his...

"Morgan?" My eyes snap up to meet his, a knowing smirk tracing the edges of his lips as I blush scarlet. Of course, he would catch me staring. But I mean...who wouldn't? The man is easy to look at.

"Ready," I choke out, wondering if he notices the

change in my voice. Owen just smiles and gestures for me to follow him farther into the gym where he's laid out a set of mats.

"Okay, so I want to begin with some stretching." When I give him a skeptical look, he rolls his eyes and sits down next to me. "I want to make sure your muscles are warmed up. I'm guessing you haven't done much weightlifting lately?" He arches his eyebrow, and I chuckle to myself as I shake my head. "That's what I thought. If you don't warm up your muscles beforehand, you'll be susceptible to pulling or tearing one when we start the actual workout." I nod, following his moves as he takes me through some basic stretches.

After ten minutes of stretching, he tells me to stand, and we do a few more things before he takes me to a treadmill.

"So, I'm going to start you off at a slow pace and increase the speed every few minutes. I want you to keep your hands on the sensors right here." He points to the handlebars in front of me, and I look at him, confused. He laughs as he takes my hands and places them on the bars. "They monitor your heart rate. I would usually take your weight and height before this, but from the panicked look you just gave me, I'm guessing you would rather not do that today." I shake my head. I know it will help him, but I'm not ready for that burst of reality yet. "That's fine. I'll just ballpark it for now." I nod as he presses a few buttons and the belt under my feet starts moving.

"So, how long did it take for you to get this place up and running?" I ask, hoping to distract myself from the fact that Owen is still shirtless, and my fingers want to run down the center of his abs and finally figure out where those v-shaped muscles lead.

"About five years. Matt and I met in College. We were both there on football scholarships and figured out pretty early that we weren't meant to go pro. This was our backup." I nod as he looks at my heart rate, types something into his phone, and then ups the speed on the treadmill. "So, what about you? Why did you leave New York? It was always your dream to live in the Big Apple and become a designer." I laugh softly to myself, remembering my dreams from high school and knowing that they crashed and burned way faster than expected.

"Turns out, you have to be good at drawing for that to work." Owen chuckles to himself, and I almost trip over my feet as he gifts me with that smirk that he always reserved for me when we were kids. Seeing it now sends shivers through my entire body.

"Want to tell me why you want to lose weight all of a sudden? I know the guy from last night said some pretty nasty things, but I also know there has to be more to it than one douche." He ups the speed one more time, and I try to catch my breath. But the longer I walk on this thing, the harder talking becomes. Owen seems to sense this and takes one last look at my heart rate and then stops the machine.

"To be honest, I've always been ashamed of my weight, even in high school." He scoffs as I get off on the machine with wobbly legs and pick my water bottle up off the floor.

"You were not fat in high school." I roll my eyes and lean against the wall, trying to catch my breath.

"You might think that, but everyone else saw something completely different. Including my fiancé back in New York, who decided to ditch me on my birthday to instead fuck a woman from work. And the best part? I walked in on them doing it in our kitchen, and he had the audacity to blame *me*. Said that without him, I was just a sad, fat girl." The moment those words come out of my mouth, Owen's face changes. His eyes narrow, and he cages me against the wall, his arms on either side of my head.

"Morgan, look at me." I audibly swallow as his face gets closer and closer to mine, causing our gazes to meet. "Are you a size two? No." My eyes lower because all I can picture is Bailey and her tiny waist and perfect arms, knowing that's Owen's type—and I am so far from that. But he surprises me because one of his hands falls from the wall and grazes the side of my thigh. I take a shuddering breath as I lift my eyes. "You are not a size two because you are a woman, Morgan. You have curves." His fingers dance along the hem of the loose shirt hanging past my hips. "And that means there's more for a man to hold onto..." His voice lowers, and a gruff-sounding growl escapes as his hand reaches under the fabric and finds the bare skin of my rib cage.

"Owen..." I murmur as his fingers grip even tighter, his lips tracing the edge of my jaw, causing my whole body to collapse against the wall behind me. "What are you doing?" I ask, not really knowing if I want to hear the answer or if I want him to continue doing exactly what he is.

He doesn't answer my question, he just leans his head against the wall beside mine, his hand traveling to my lower back and pulling me against him.

"I know you wore this shirt to hide from me." I gasp as his fingers grip the softness of my skin. "I want you to know that what's under this shirt is nothing to hide, baby. It's fucking sexy as hell." My heart leaps into my throat as my mouth opens to say something, anything, but no sound comes out. Did Owen just tell me he thinks I'm sexy? That can't be right...can it?

Before I have a chance to ask him what he means, his phone goes off, pulling us both out of the moment. He looks down at the caller ID, and groans. "I gotta take this. Give me a sec, okay?" I nod silently, not having the words to explain the feelings coursing through my body.

This just got interesting.

11

OWEN

"*W*hat do you want, Bailey?" I mutter, looking behind me to make sure Morgan can't hear me. Of course, I would get this call the second I get my hands on the one woman I've been dreaming about since I was sixteen.

"Is that any way to say hello to your girlfriend?" she says in what I know she thinks is her sexy voice, but right now, it only irritates the fuck out of me.

"Bailey, you know you're not my girlfriend anymore. What do you want?" I don't hide the curt tone of my voice as she huffs on the other end.

"Whatever. I wanted to see if I could come by tomorrow and take some pictures for Instagram." Is she serious? She called me for this? I almost throw my phone against the wall but stop myself.

"Bailey, you know what my answer's gonna be."

"Come on, Owen, you never had a problem before!" she whines. I roll my eyes and glance back at Morgan, who looks at me with a sweet expression on her face. I give her a wink and smile, and a blush travels up her neck, cresting over her cheeks. *Fuck, she's gorgeous.* It's a shame she doesn't see it.

"That's because you were my girlfriend before. Now, you're not. And I'm not okay with you mooching off my business. If you want gym pictures, I know a few guys that would be more than willing to help you out. But it won't be me." She starts huffing again, so I stop it in its tracks. "Bails, we're over. You either accept it or don't. Regardless, just know that we're done, and that means I'm done catering to your demands, too." I disconnect from the call abruptly and hope that's the last time I hear from her. But knowing Bailey, I figure I'll have a few more months of torture until I get some semblance of peace.

I turn and see Morgan taking a drink from her water bottle. I smile, motioning for her to follow me to the weights. I set her up, and we do a few reps of triceps curls, some shoulder presses, and then finally, I get her down on a mat and in position to do a plank.

"You have gotta be kidding me. You hate me, don't you?" she mutters as she gets in the position and I pull out my phone and set the timer.

"It's not that bad," I say, smiling because I know she's going to say something sarcastic back.

"Yeah, maybe for you, Hercules. But for us mere mortals, it's not that simple." I burst out laughing because this is the Morgan I knew all those years ago. The one that gave as good as she got—and without hesitation.

"I just want to see what you can do. All of these exercises are for me to get a baseline. That way, the more we train, the more I can see your progress." She gives me a skeptical look as I motion for her to get ready. "Okay, we're starting in five, four, three, two, one. Go!" She gets into the plank position, and I watch her. She struggles from the onset, and I'm not surprised. Most people can't plank for longer than a few seconds the first time they do it, so when she collapses at fifteen seconds, I'm thoroughly impressed. "Morgan, that was amazing!" I shout as she looks up at me like I'm talking gibberish.

"What the hell are you watching over there? I didn't even make it to thirty seconds!" She struggles to catch her breath, so I lean over and grab her water bottle as she reaches for it and takes a sip.

"Morgan, most people can't do thirty seconds the first time they do a plank. You should be proud." She takes a deep breath, and after a few heartbeats, a genuine smile crosses her face.

"Really?" I give her a reassuring smile and nod my head.

"Are you ready to go again?"

"Again? You really fucking hate me, don't you?" I laugh as she gets back into position.

"I don't hate you. The exact opposite, actually." She stills, and I try to ignore the awkward silence. "This time, I want you to try and beat your last time, okay? Think you can do that?" She nods, eyes still focused on the mat, and I curse myself for opening my big mouth. I quickly shake myself out of it and reset the timer. "Ready? In five, four, three, two, one!" She holds herself in position and, right away, I notice this time is harder, just like I expected. Her arms are shaking under her weight, and her face contorts the more time passes. Before the fifteen seconds are up, she collapses into a heap on the mat.

"Did I beat the time?" she asks, and for a split second, I think about lying, telling her she did. But the trainer in me knows that won't help.

"No. But that's okay. We know you can do fifteen seconds, which is amazing for a beginner. Now we can improve from there, okay?" I can see the disappointment on her face as I help her up. "Morgan, you won't be good at all of this right away. I never expected you to be. All I expect is for you to try your best. That's it. Okay?" She nods, taking a swig from her water bottle.

"What's next?" she says through haggard breathing, and I smile. Because no matter the outcome of this training, I know I will make her see the woman I do.

After an hour's workout, Morgan looks thoroughly exhausted. And honestly, I'm beat, too. I tried to do as many of the things with her as I could, just so she wasn't doing them alone, and I realized early on that I haven't done that in a long time.

"You want to do this again tomorrow?" I ask, but she looks at me as if I just asked her to sell drugs to a cop.

"Are you insane? I'm going to be so sore tomorrow. I don't know how I'm going to survive my boss's visit." I give her a guilty smile and toss her a towel, watching as she wipes the sweat from her forehead.

"Well, what about the day after? It will give you a chance to heal a bit, and I'll make sure to change up the routine so we work different muscles." She thinks about it for a second and then smiles.

"Sure, sounds good. Same time?"

"Yup. Seems to work for both of us." She nods her head as she gathers her bag and heads for the front door.

"Hey, wait. Let me walk you to your car."

"You don't have to do that," she says, but I just give her a look that says I'm doing it anyway and that she should accept it.

When the cold air hits me, I take a deep breath as Morgan leads me towards her car that's parked directly in front of Hello Beautiful Boutique. Before she gets in, I take her arm and spin her to face me.

"What are you doing?" she asks as she leans against the car. It takes every ounce of my control not to take her lips right here like I wanted to in the gym, back before Bailey ruined everything.

"I want to let you know that I'm proud of you." That's not what I wanted to say exactly. What I *want* to say is that I think she's the most beautiful woman I have ever seen, and that the idea of not kissing her is driving me crazy. But I hold back.

"Proud of me for sweating through this shirt and making a fool of myself?" she says jokingly, but I see a sliver of truth in her gaze. I shake my head.

"M, what you did tonight was amazing. You gave 100% on everything I threw at you, and that is something to be proud of." She rolls her eyes, and I realize I can't handle being this far away from her anymore. I take a step toward her and cup her face in my hands. "Nothing happens overnight. Take today as a win, okay?" She nods, but I also see desire flare in her eyes. Before I do something really stupid like tell her how perfect I think she is, or how sexy she looks all flushed and leaning her head back to meet my eyes, I lean forward and place a soft kiss on her forehead. Her intake of breath and shuddering exhale tells me everything I need to know. So I lean in and whisper one last thing in her ear. "I'll see you later, superstar."

I don't wait for a response before giving her one last smile and making my way back to the gym. Just as I'm about to head inside, Morgan calls my name. When I turn, she's standing in the exact spot I left her in.

"Thank you," she says so softly I barely hear her. I nod and give her one last wink.

"Anytime, gorgeous." And with that, I head back inside and hope that this is the start of Morgan realizing that she is enough.

MORGAN

"So, you're telling me that man put his hands on you, told you he thinks you're sexy, and almost kissed you...and you haven't jumped his bones yet?" Allie has been sitting on my couch for the last twenty minutes, listening as I explain everything that's happened over the last few weeks. Her flight came in right on time, and even though she insisted on staying at a hotel, I made her use one of my spare bedrooms. I mean, the girl did give me a job, and she's one of my best friends.

"It's more complicated than that, and you know it." She pulls her dark hair into a messy bun on the top of her head and crosses her legs on the couch.

"Morgan, you need to stop letting the past cloud what could happen in your future. You know I can get Ben on the phone right now, and he'll talk your ear off about knowing your worth…" I don't answer her, just throw a pillow at her head. "Hey! That was uncalled for," she says through laughter as I join her.

"I know you love your husband, but do not bring him into this!" I point my finger as I head into the kitchen to get another bottle of wine. As I make my way back into the room, she gives me a sad smile.

"What's this really about?" Fuck. She's way too good at reading me, and I know I won't get out of this until I spill it.

"I went on a date," I blurt out. Allie's eyes bulge as she sits up straight and gets a giddy look on her face.

"What? Why is this the first time I'm hearing of this?" I shake my head, taking a swig of wine before settling and bracing myself for the onslaught of questions.

"I was set up, it wasn't my idea," I point out, but she just motions for me to continue as if that part of the story doesn't matter. "Fine. So, I went out with him, and he decided to spend the entire night commenting on the amount of food I ate and telling me I should lose weight."

"Shit…" she groans as she gets up, puts down her glass on the coffee table in front of us, and sits beside me. "That's shitty, sweetie, but you know it's not true, right?" I give her the side-eye, and she lightly smacks my leg. "Morgan, you are gorgeous just the way you are. And from what you've told me, Owen thinks so, too." I roll my eyes because even though Owen has expressed interest, more than once, the idea still doesn't seem plausible.

"You're insane," I murmur, hoping she lets up. But she doesn't.

"Morgan, look at me." I do, and she gives me those big hazel eyes that, in college, got us so many free drinks. "I know I won't be able to change your mind right now. And as much as I would love to just send you to one of Ben's retreats,"—I give her a contrite look that makes her laugh—"I know it won't work. The only way for you to get past this is to accept yourself. And if that means working out and losing weight? Then I'm here for it. Whatever you need."

"You know, despite how much you try and push your husband on me, you're a great friend." I stick out my tongue as we both laugh until we can't anymore.

"I love you. You know that, right? No matter what you look like." A small, shy smile crosses my lips as I lean my head on her shoulder and feel her arm wrap around me.

"And I love you despite how good you always look," I joke, sending us both into another fit of laughter. I don't know what I would do without her in my life.

* * *

"MORGAN, THIS PLACE LOOKS AMAZING," Allie says in awe as her eyes scan the room, taking in my displays. And just like I thought she would, she goes straight to the shoe display. "God, every time I see these shoes, they call to me." She holds one of the new Louboutins I brought in last week. They are velvet with small gunmetal spikes all around the edge—and, of course, the signature red sole.

"They are amazing." Allie takes the display and holds it in front of her face and then glances at the price tag. I start to laugh. "Allie, I know you know how much those shoes cost." She starts to shake her head and then laughs.

"Oh, I know how much they cost. I'm calculating how much groveling I'll have to do when Ben sees them in my suitcase." I chuckle as Brooke unlocks the front door and looks around the room.

"We're officially open!" she says, and to my surprise, we have a line of about ten women standing outside. And just like that, our day flies by. I spend most of the day greeting customers along with Allie, who convinces more than one woman to invest in a good pair of shoes while Becca mans the checkout line. Before I have a chance to breathe, I look at my watch and see that it's past four in the afternoon, and it's our first lull of the day.

"Holy shit," I mutter just as Allie comes over and gives me the biggest hug ever, rocking us back and forth.

"That was insane and the best six hours of my life." We both laugh, looking around at the decimated shelves that I've tried to restock throughout the day. I still notice some holes.

"Honey, this place looks amazing!" my mom calls from across the room, and I give her a big smile. My father follows her as he always does, and they both come toward me and give me a big hug.

"We're so proud of you, honey," Dad says, letting me go and moving to Allie. "Allie Baker, it's so good to see you again." Allie has her hand out as if my father is going to shake it, but I laugh because I know what is about to happen. He pushes the hand away and brings her in for a hug. "Family always gets a hug. And since you've been so loyal to our girl, you are now family." Allie looks at me, and I shrug.

"Thank you so much, Mr. Lawson."

"Please, call me James. And you remember my wife, Diana," he says, motioning to my mother, who I know is trying to hold back tears.

"Yes, of course. Good to see you again, Diana." My mother also brings Allie in for a hug, and I have to laugh at how uncomfortable my friend looks.

"Okay, I think that's enough hugging for now." Allie gives me a grateful look as my mother lets her go and starts to look around.

"You really have done a wonderful job, honey." I start to blush, and Allie comes to stand beside me, her arm around my waist.

"She really did. I picked the right girl," she says, looking at me and winking.

As I make my way to the front of the store, trying to get away from all the attention, the bell chimes, and I see a huge shadow pass through the door. When I look up, my breath catches at the sight of Owen in his signature basketball shorts, white t-shirt and running shoes. His baseball hat is on backwards, allowing me full view of those eyes that make me weak in the knees, no matter how much I try to fight it.

"What are you doing here?" I ask, hoping Allie and my parents don't spot us and come right over.

My eyes scan the place and I see that she's nowhere to be found. I breathe a sigh of relief.

"I wanted to come over and see how you're doing. There's been a steady stream of people all day. Congrats." I pray the blush doesn't make an appearance, but the minute he flashes me a smile, it starts creeping up my neck. Our eyes meet, and I swear I see a flicker of hunger there. But before I have a chance to dwell on it, it's gone.

"Yeah, it's been a crazy day for sure. But it seems like it was a success." He nods and starts to look around. "Are you looking for something?" I ask, veiling the curiosity as much as possible.

"Yeah, my mom's birthday is coming up, and I wanted to see what you have." My eyes dart around the store, and honestly, our stock is decimated. He turns and gives me a wink that makes me stop in my tracks. "Maybe it wasn't such a good idea to come once everyone else has emptied the place, huh?" I shrug, not really finding the words. Just as I'm about to take him to the other side of the store, I feel a presence behind me. Allie.

"You must be Owen." I silently curse the gods for what is about to happen. He nods and takes her hand. "I'm Allie, the owner."

"Ah, so you're the one that got Morgan to

come home finally." Allie nods her head, still holding his hand until I elbow her, and she drops it, giving me that innocent look I know isn't innocent at all. "Well, thank you. We missed her around here."

"We? Or just you?" Allie asks, and my intake of breath makes them both look my way.

"Allie! Seriously? You're here two days and already meddling where you shouldn't." I roll my eyes as Owen smiles down at us.

"I have five siblings. It's my job to meddle. If I don't, I learn nothing." I dismiss her flippant comment and turn to Owen.

"If you come back tomorrow, I should have some more stuff put out. I can help you find something for your mom then." He gives me that panty-melting smile as he leans in and kisses my cheek. The feel of his lips on my skin is a sensation I wish I never knew. Because right now? It's all I want to feel. As Owen makes his way to the door, Allie comes to stand beside me, her hand taking mine and squeezing so hard I swear she's trying to break every finger I have.

"Oh, Morgan?" Owen says, turning at the door and meeting my gaze. "I'm glad you're home." And with that, he leaves, the door chiming as Allie and I watch him walk down the sidewalk and into his gym.

"Girl, you are in so much trouble," Allie whispers, and I sigh because she's right.

"Honey, was that Owen I just saw leave?" my mother calls from across the room. I shut my eyes and pray this doesn't become a thing. Allie gives me a look and happily leaves the awkwardness for the storage room. I wish I could follow her.

"Yes, he works next door. He's a personal trainer." My mother is known for not being able to mask her feelings, no matter how much she tries to embody the epitome of Southern charm.

"Well, he should stay away after what he did to you." My heart sinks at the mention of that night. Sometimes when I look at him now, all I see is the teenage boy who broke my heart, but then other times, I see the man he grew into and have this unbearable need to know who he is today.

"Mom, that was ten years ago. We were both kids," I say, hoping she'll let it go. But, of course, that's asking too much.

"Ten years doesn't make up for the fact that I had to listen to you cry yourself to sleep for weeks until you moved away." I cringe, not knowing she knew. I thought I was being discreet. "But if you're trying to mend fences, then by all means. I will stay out of it." I know that's a lie, but I appreciate the effort.

"Thanks, Mom, love you."

"Love you, too, sweetie. Your father and I are so proud of you and happy that you're home." I can't help the tears that fall, and she brings me in for a hug.

"I'm happy I'm home too, Mom." If only I could convince my brain that being here is the right thing for my heart. Because having Owen this close is messing with my head.

13

OWEN

*I*t's been a month since Morgan and I started working out together, making my resolve to keep my hands to myself a lot harder the more time we spend together. When my phone goes off beside me, I pick it up thinking it's Morgan texting that she can't make her training tonight, since she's done that a few times over these last few weeks since her shop's been so busy, but it's not. It's Bailey with yet another essay, explaining why we were so good together and that I should rethink my decision to break up with her. I know I should block her number. It's what Matt thinks I should do. But for some reason, I feel bad. As if letting her rant at me over text once every week is my punishment for stringing her along for so long when I knew I wasn't happy. I don't even read the message before I delete it, setting my phone down on the counter as my eyes scan the front door, waiting for Morgan to arrive.

It only takes a few minutes before the front door opens, and a wave of heat enters the room. Morgan makes her way in, walks right past me without so much as a word, and heads straight for the changing room. Odd. She usually says something to me on her way past, but I just dismiss it and head into the workout space to set up the mats and weights. It only takes her about five minutes to get changed. When she comes back out, she's dressed in her usual yoga pants and a large t-shirt that shows off her one shoulder and the fact that she's wearing a fluorescent yellow sports bra underneath. The color accents her tanned skin, making her blond hair somehow brighter, and her blue eyes shine even more as they focus on me.

"You ready?" I ask since she still hasn't said a word. She shrugs and slowly walks over to the mats. "Hey, you okay?" My voice is soft as I walk toward her. The minute I try to place a hand on her shoulder, she shrinks away.

"I'm fine," she grunts as she gets on the floor and begins stretching. We go through a few exercises in total silence, and the longer we sit here together, the more I feel the anger, unease, and frustration flowing off her. But she refuses to talk.

Just as we start the last stretch, she finally speaks up.

"Why are we doing so many stretches? This doesn't help me. I need to run. I need to sweat. I need to feel the fat falling off my body, Owen," All of these words are said through clenched teeth, and when she won't meet my gaze, I stop what I'm doing and sit beside her.

"What's going on?" I ask, hoping I'll finally figure out what's really going through her head.

Morgan's back slumps, and when her eyes meet mine, they are full of unshed tears. "We've been doing this for a month, and I've only lost five pounds." Her voice hitches as she tries her hardest to keep those tears from falling, but a few escapes and I use that as an excuse to touch her, trailing my thumbs down her cheeks and wiping away the evidence.

"M, that's normal. Losing a pound a week is the best way to safely lose weight, and the best scenario for success." I'm not lying to placate her; I'm not saying these things to make her feel better. I'm actually trying to tell her that what she's doing is working, even if she doesn't think it is.

"I don't give a shit if it's normal. It's been thirty days, and I still look the fucking same!" She stands, her voice rising with every word that leaves her mouth. I take a deep breath, wanting nothing more than to go over there and hold her. But right now, the anger that radiates off her body lets me know that is probably the worst idea. I hate the self-loathing I see in her eyes. I hate the way she picks apart every aspect of her body because people in this world can't get past what the media deems *acceptable*. It's a bunch of bullshit, and I've tried to build my brand around making women feel good in their skin, no matter what that looks like. But right now, Morgan is angry, and I know nothing the trainer in me can say will change her mind. So, I decide to talk to her not as her trainer, but as the man who's still in love with her.

"Morgan, there is *nothing* wrong with you." She scoffs and turns away, and that's when everything comes to a head.

"It's not working! I need it to go faster! I need you to push me harder!" Her voice pitches higher as her arms outstretch, and she waves them around as if that will get her point across better. I've seen this before. Many times. And each time is different. Sometimes, my clients just want quick results.

Sometimes they want to be exactly who someone else wants them to be and fast. But most of the time, it's internal. And from the tears continuing to fall from Morgan's eyes now, I know it's the latter. I just need to get it out of her.

"Why does it need to go faster, M? What is so time-sensitive that you need to transform yourself so quickly?" She doesn't answer as her gaze moves to the floor. I tilt up her chin so her eyes meets mine. Everything changes in that instant. Her body goes slack, and all the tension leaves her shoulders as if what she's been carrying around is more than she can bear. But it's not until my hand finds her shaking one, our fingers twining, and the pressure of her fingers squeezes mine that it dawns on me how much this girl is hurting.

"I don't want to hate the person I see in the mirror anymore." *Fucking hell.* My heart sinks to the floor as Morgan's eyes catch mine. My hands move of their own accord and cup the sides of her face.

"Baby, no. Do not hate that woman, because she's beautiful." She shuts her eyes, shaking her head vehemently. I wish with every fiber of my being that my words could heal the wounds inside her, but I know they won't.

"No. No, I'm not." The tears fall freely now as her

eyes stay closed. I wipe away the moisture and lean my forehead against hers.

"Morgan, loving yourself is more important than what anyone thinks of you. I promise it will get easier," I whisper, hoping some of the words make their way through the wall she's built around herself.

"Why couldn't I have been born looking like Bailey?" she mumbles, and I know she means every word. I can't do this anymore. I can't take the thought of her comparing herself to Bailey, and I can't tiptoe around my feelings anymore. I'm done ignoring how my heart starts beating uncontrollably when she walks into a room, and I'm done letting her think that she isn't better than Bailey just because she's a different size.

"Morgan, stop. I need you to listen to me. You are not ugly. You are not fat. And you shouldn't compare yourself to someone like Bailey because she doesn't hold a candle to you!" My voice growls with every word, and before she can say anything, I pull her face to mine and seal my lips to hers.

Damn.

I didn't know it would feel like this. The fantasy I had concocted over the years of what it would feel like to kiss Morgan doesn't even come close to the real thing. Before I have a chance to overthink things, I lift her off the floor, pinning her against the mirrored wall behind us.

"Owen, what are you doing?" She moans as my lips travel down her neck and suck on the skin right under her ear. I smile, chuckling because if she's questioning what I'm doing right now, I'm not as good as I thought.

"I'd have thought it was pretty obvious..." I murmur as my hands start to wander, slipping under her shirt to grip her hips. Her head falls back against the wall in pleasure. "But if you still don't understand, maybe I should explain." My lips attack hers once more, and I bask in the way her body melts against me.

"What the fuck?!" We break apart, Morgan dropping to the floor and fixing her shirt since it seems I hiked it up past her chest. I turn around and face the one person I know could ruin the very thing I want the most.

Bailey.

"What are you doing here, Bails?" I demand, stepping in front of Morgan, knowing what's about to happen and hoping I can deflect as much as possible.

"What the fuck are you doing with that whale? You seriously broke up with me for that?" Her face scrunches in disgust as she points in Morgan's direction. Delicate fingers grip the sides of my shirt as I feel Morgan's head fall forward and rest against my spine. My hand discreetly falls behind me as my fingers grip hers, hoping it helps with the barrage of hate that I know is coming.

"Bailey. You know you're not welcome here. Please leave." My voice is hard and stern, but I'm trying hard not to sink to her level. Given the way Morgan's fingers grip mine, I'm starting to wonder why.

Before Bailey can say anything else, I turn and face Morgan. I see the uncertainty in her eyes and wonder what I have to do to make sure that look never crosses her face again. "You doing okay?" I say, my fingers brushing the sides of her face as I smile. She leans into my touch and nods, but I don't believe her.

"What is she doing here?" Morgan's voice is below a whisper, and I don't know what to say. *I'm sorry my ex is insane and is a raging bitch? I'm sorry I'm a chickenshit and haven't told her to fuck off yet? I'm sorry I waited all these years to finally show you how I feel?*

"Hello! I'm still standing here, you know!" Bailey screeches. I turn my head, and our eyes meet.

"Yes, I see that. Care to tell me why exactly you

came into my place of business when you know you aren't welcome?" Bailey recoils. I've never been this harsh before, and I know it's actually a few weeks too late.

"You didn't think that a few weeks ago when we fucked using that pull-up machine..." Bailey points beside her, and the intake of breath behind me sets my teeth on edge. It takes everything in me not to lunge at her and shove her through the door.

"Uh, I'm gonna go change..." Morgan whispers, and before I can tell her not to, she's gone.

"You seriously like her fat ass more than mine?" Bailey sputters, watching Morgan as she closes the door to the changing rooms. "I mean, you went from a ten to a minus ten if you ask me." She chuckles at her bad joke as I shake my head.

"You need to leave, Bailey," I say, checking the door to make sure Morgan hasn't come back out. I don't want her to be anywhere near this. "Now. Before I call the cops on you for trespassing." She rolls her eyes and leans back against the front counter.

"You would do that to the girl you said you loved not even four weeks ago?" She starts to undo the skin-tight hoodie covering her chest, revealing a black bra that leaves nothing to the imagination.

"Fucking hell. Cover yourself before you embar-rass yourself," I mutter, turning back toward the changing room door, glad to see Morgan is still safely on the other side. Bailey barks out a laugh before fully taking off the hoodie and standing in front of me in just her bra and jeans.

"I have nothing to be embarrassed about. But your chubby friend in there? She could never live up to this." She gestures to her body, clearly thinking that will win me over when it's doing the exact opposite. "She'll never get you so hard you have to fuck her in your office in the middle of the day. She'll never know what it feels like to have you fuck her like you can't get enough because you love fucking girls like me, not girls like her," she spits, pointing at the door that is now open, Morgan standing there with wide eyes.

Fuck.

"Morgan, it's not true…" I start, but she holds up her hand. When our eyes lock, my stomach sinks at the sight of the tears threatening to fall.

"Oh, isn't that sweet? Did I hurt her feelings?" Bailey says with a shit-eating grin on her face, clearly satisfied with the hurt she inflicted.

"I'm done," Morgan says as she picks up her bag from the floor and heads to the front door. "You might want to put a shirt on," she suggests to Bailey as she passes. "Don't want people getting the wrong idea." I give Morgan a small smile, wishing I could wrap her in my arms and shield her from all of this. But I know right now the best thing to do is get her as far away from Bailey as possible. Even if that means being far away from *me*.

"I'll call you later," I say before Morgan heads out the door. I expect a slight nod, maybe a smile. What I don't expect is the look of defeat.

"I don't think that's a good idea. I need some time." And before I have a chance to fight, she's gone, leaving me alone with the one person standing in the way of my happiness.

14

MORGAN

*I*t doesn't take long for the tears to come the moment I get into my car and make my way home. I can't figure out if they're from heartache, frustration, or just plain anger. I don't know what it is about Bailey that makes me want to punch her perfect face until she understands what her words do to people like me. Those who don't have the self-confidence to brush it off as if it's nothing. People who take every single letter of every single word and store it away in a little box in our minds for when we're feeling horrible about ourselves.

Fat ass.

You don't love girls like her. You love girls like me.

You loved me a few weeks ago.

All of those things run through my head as I drive aimlessly through the city, wondering what the hell I'm going to do. I mean, before that moment? Before Bailey walked in and ruined everything, I felt like the luckiest girl in the world. Owen kissed me. And not just a friendly peck, a bruiser that left me panting and wanting much, much more. But what I'm left with now is doubt and a sack full of unanswered questions. Why now? Why is he making a move now when he's had weeks to do it? Why did he say he loved me in high school that night by the beach and then never bring it up again? Why am I afraid of the answers to those questions? Because I know in the end, those answers will turn the world I know upside down. And right now, I can't figure out if that's a good thing.

When I park in my driveway, I don't get out. I sit there, staring at my phone and knowing I have to hit the call button. So, I do it before I change my mind.

"Hello!" Allie says cheerfully, and I open my mouth to say something but I'm speechless. How do I explain to her what happened when I don't even know what that is. "Morgan? You there?" she asks as a hint of worry enters her tone.

"Yeah, I'm here. Sorry, must have spaced out there for a bit." I try to mask the hitch in my voice because the tears are still steadily streaming down my cheeks, making it hard to concentrate on anything but breathing through the weight that seems to have settled on my chest.

"Fuck, what happened?" Allie asks as I hear a muffled voice and then a door shutting, leaving us in silence. I honestly don't know what I would do without her. When I left New York, I never thought about what it would be like to move thousands of miles away from everything I knew, including the friends I thought I'd have for life. Turns out friendships are hard to manage from a distance, and everyone I knew just fell away. Except for Allie. She's been a constant, a source of never-ending friendship that doesn't seem to diminish, no matter the length of time between texts or the number of miles separating us. And right now, I wish more than anything that she was here and not in New Orleans.

It doesn't take long for me to spill my guts about everything: my frustration over losing weight, the kiss that might have changed everything, and of course...Bailey.

"That fucking bitch." Allie swears as I sit alone in

my car, tears streaming down my face with her on speakerphone.

"Yeah, well, she's not wrong," I say. Allie groans as if what I just said is the most outrageous thing she's ever heard.

"Morgan, did you listen to yourself when you told me the story just now? Did you miss the fact that Owen pushed you up against a wall and kissed the hell out of you? Or did you just forget?" Of course, I didn't forget, that part is seared into my brain.

"What if Bailey's right? What if Owen can't like a girl like me because he's used to girls like her?"

"Have you actually talked to him? Maybe ask him these questions." Damn her and her logic.

"Of course, I haven't. That would be the reasonable thing to do. Since when do I do that? And plus, how do I go about starting that kind of conversation? Ask: Why do you like me? How can you like someone like me when you went out with someone like Bailey?"

"Yes, exactly that."

"You make it sound so easy. None of this is easy."

"Morgan, all of this should be simple. You've known Owen since you were kids. This shouldn't be something you hesitate about. From the little time I spent with him, I saw the way his eyes followed you through a room, the way his body always turned toward you the minute you entered. He gives you the same look that Ben gives me when he's about to tell me he loves me. That boy is crazy about you, and you need to either talk to him or stop stringing him along." God, she's right. She's always freaking right.

"Why do you always have the answers? Why can't you be as lost as me?"

"Because I was you before I met Ben. You need to learn to accept yourself. Maybe then you'll trust Owen enough to let him love you."

"You've been spending too much time with your husband," I joke, but her words burn into the back of my mind. This might be harder than I thought.

Getting off the phone with Allie, I make my way inside. Just as I close the door and head into the kitchen, I hear a knock. I know who it is before I even open it, and I am not in the mood.

"Owen, I really don't think you being here is a good idea," I say through the door, not opening it.

"Can you please talk to me? That's all I ask." I take a deep breath and decide that maybe talking to him will get me some answers. So, I open the door. Before I even have a chance to say a word, Owen pushes into the house to cup the sides of my face and plants his lips on mine.

I wasn't expecting this. I wasn't expecting to feel like this again. But the longer his lips ravage mine, and I hear the groan that leaves his mouth...the minute I wrap my arms around his neck, I melt. I know we should talk. I know that I need answers before this goes any further, but right now, I only want to bask in the sensation of his lips against mine, his hands gripping my hips, and the feel of his cock hardening against my stomach. Because in the back of my mind, I know this can all go away in a split second if I allow it. The idea that someone like Owen is attached to someone like me doesn't work. It doesn't look the way it's supposed to, and once that thought plants itself in my brain, it's like being doused in cold water. Using my hands to push him away from me physically, my fingers immediately find my lips and I miss his taste instantly.

"We need to talk, right?" My chest is heaving, my hands shaking as my mind tries its hardest not to think about what those lips can do. But when Owen's eyes bore into mine, moving from my lips to my eyes, it takes all of my strength to stay away.

"Yeah...talk," he rumbles as I lead us through the house, feeling his eyes on me the entire time. Everything is different. When he kissed me the first time, I thought if it ended, everything could go back to normal. After that last one, after feeling the desperation in his touch and lips, I realize that nothing will be the same. No matter what the outcome.

15

MORGAN

The second we sit on the couch, the awkwardness sets in. I have no idea what to do with my hands. I pull at the fabric of my shirt, making sure it flows over my knees. Owen avoids my eyes, simply stares at the floor as if he weren't just kissing the fuck out of me, as if his hands weren't all over my body a second ago.

"What did you want to talk about?" I ask, my voice cracking as my gaze stays focused on the t-shirt wrapped around my crossed legs. When Owen doesn't say anything, I look over and see his eyes are still focused on the floor. "Owen?" I say a bit louder. His head pops up, a small smile playing at the corners of his lips. "What did you want to talk about?" I repeat as he starts shaking his head.

"I wish I could go back and change everything," he declares as my brow furrows in confusion.

"What do you mean?" Owen's face lifts, his eyes looking into mine as he shifts to face me.

"I wish I could go back to prom night. Tell Kelly to go fuck herself and do what I was planning to do." My heart starts to race, my hands turning clammy as I open my mouth to ask what he's talking about. But nothing comes out. "I know you remember what I said a few weeks ago at the beach. I know we've kind of pushed it to the side because neither of us was ready to deal with what I said. But I'm ready now, and I need you to know some things."

I have never been so aware of how loudly I breathe. The room gets eerily silent as I wait for Owen to start talking.

"Prom night was supposed to be the night I told you I loved you." I take a shaky breath as Owen gives me a shy smile and then continues. "I was in love with you for a while, probably ever since our epic scary movie night sophomore year that had you hiding under my arm the entire time. Having you in my arms that night, feeling you nestled against me for protection from something, even imaginary things, changed everything." He arches an eyebrow because he knows I'll fight to the death to defend that ghosts are real. "It made me realize that I wanted to feel like that all the time.

"After that, everything changed for me. I couldn't see you as just a friend anymore. I only saw the goofy, smiley, beautiful girl that I wanted to make happy." I frown because the way he's describing me is the exact opposite of how I saw myself at that time. High school wasn't horrible for me, but it wasn't a cakewalk, either. I got the glances in the hall, the snickers in gym class when I struggled to keep up with everyone else, and of course, the evil looks when Owen and I walked down the hall together. Yet, I try not to remember those moments. I attempt to remember that Owen made me feel accepted with the way he always made sure I was okay, even when he didn't have to—and especially the way he made me feel as if I was the only important person in the room.

Even then, I knew I loved Owen. Maybe it was only in that teenage way that always seems so incredibly consuming in the moment. However, it still felt incredibly fragile as if everything were just some dream I concocted out of thin air to help myself cope with everything around me.

It wasn't until prom that I realized the illusion was just that: an illusion. Reality came crashing down, and I learned that even if someone showed you their best side, the opposite could happen just as fast. Owen's eyes track me as I grapple with the words he's saying, but it's only when his hand reaches over and rests lightly on mine that our eyes lock.

"I know your version of that night is vastly different from mine, and I'm so sorry for that. I want you to know that everything I did was to protect you." I roll my eyes, sick and tired of hearing that from someone who was supposed to be my best friend. Instead, he became my worst enemy, all in the span of one night.

"Protect me? Is that what you thought you were doing? Because what you did was destroy me. It took me years to get over that betrayal. It took me *years* of ignoring memories of you for me to finally move past that night..." What I don't say is that prom night changed me. It made me realize that I couldn't dream of being with someone like Owen because boys like him weren't meant for girls like me. Society never understands that. I mean, for God's sake, there's probably a reality show about a fat girl with a hot guy. I shudder at the thought of the judgement passed on to not only the woman but also the man for *settling* for someone society deems beneath him.

"Morgan, I spent most of prom night trying to convince Kelly not to humiliate you for the rest of the year. She knew how I felt about you. I don't know how, but she did. And she used those feelings to make me do whatever she wanted. Was I wrong to follow her? Yes. If I could go back and do it all over, I'd ignore her and just protect you, no matter what she tried to do. But I was young, and I thought I was doing the right thing."

"So, she was blackmailing you?" I ask, confused because none of this makes sense. Owen nods, waiting for everything he said to sink in. "You're telling me that Kelly, the captain of the cheerleading squad, found out that you had feelings for me and used that to get you to stand me up on prom night?" I can hear my disbelief. Because it doesn't seem plausible. In my mind, the Owen from high school didn't have feelings for me. He didn't want to love me. He just wanted to be my friend. So, differentiating between the Owen I thought I knew and the Owen that is being presented to me now, is hard.

"You don't believe me," he states, his hand falling away as he stands and starts to pace around the room. I just sit there, wondering where the hell we go from here. "Even after that first kiss—hell, even after that kiss a few minutes ago—you still can't understand that I'm attracted to you?" His voice sounds agitated, and that's the moment my wall extends even higher. Nope. Not happening.

"Can you blame me? I was in love with you in high school, and you ditched me. Never speaking to me again." He goes to say something, but I stop him. "Then I went to college and tried my best to get over you, and what did I do then? I fell for the first guy that batted an eye in my direction. He ended up asking me to marry him, only to sleep with his secretary the night of my birthday party!" I scream, feeling my chest compress as the weight of what I'm saying hits me. I didn't mean to blurt out all my baggage about Aaron, but it came out faster than I could control it. The fury in Owen's eyes makes me step back, but a second later, his gaze softens, allowing me to relax a bit.

"I didn't want to stop talking to you, but you ignored me whenever I tried. *And* you moved away right after graduation." His arms become more animated the more frustrated he gets. "I even tried to get your parents to tell me where you went, but they wouldn't say a word." I say a silent prayer and then thank them for that.

"It doesn't matter, it's in the past," I mutter, trying to get past him, needing some space that doesn't include his presence. But Owen just shakes his head, gently grabbing my arm and holding me in place.

"No, it's not. Morgan, don't you get it?" I look at him, confused.

"Get what?" The second the question is out of my mouth, he's on me, his mouth on mine. Yet this time, it's different. It's not rushed or bruising. It's gentle, soft, and all-consuming to the point where I forget what we were talking about. When our lips part, he holds my face steady in his hands as our eyes lock.

"Do you get it yet?" I shake my head, just wanting to feel his lips on mine once more. And from the smirk on his face, Owen has caught on to my plan. "M, you have always been my endgame. Even when we were apart, I thought of you all the time. I never forgave myself for what I did that night, but I knew that if and when I saw you next, I wouldn't waste the opportunity." His lips lightly graze mine, a whisper of a touch compared to the two previous times he touched me.

"But—" I begin. He shakes his head and holds a finger to my lips.

"No, I don't want to hear any of that right now. Right now, I just want to show you. Because, obviously, words are not working." The second those words leave his mouth, the air in the room changes, and my head falls back as his lips find purchase on my skin once more. "Words will come later. Right now, I just want you to feel. Okay, baby?" I shiver, secretly loving the nickname I always wished he'd call me.

Before I have a chance to grasp what he means, his lips are on mine, and he attacks me with more passion than any of the previous make out sessions we've had combined. My hands delve into his blond hair, his backwards hat falling to the floor as his tongue demands entrance to my mouth. Every single doubt I had flies out the window as his hands travel past my hips and land on my ass. He lifts me, pinning me to the wall behind us.

The groan that leaves my throat echoes through the room as Owen's lips trail down my neck, leaving me boneless in their wake. "M, you have no idea how long I've wanted to do this..." he grunts into my skin as my head falls back against the wall and I try to let those words soak in. Before I have a chance to over-think what he said, and what all of this means for us, Owen takes one of his hands and cups the side of my face, bringing my eyes to his. "I know we still have a lot to talk about. But right now, I just want it to be us, like this. Okay?" I nod because the idea of stopping whatever this is doesn't seem plausible to me.

His breath cascades over my skin as he kisses the shell of my ear, sending shivers up my spine. My hips move, searching for friction. Owen wraps his arm around my back, pulling me away from the wall as he walks us slowly across the room.

"Owen, put me down, I'm too heavy," I whisper against him, not wanting him to listen to me but still worried, nonetheless.

"Stop. You weigh less than what I bench press on a light day, so get those thoughts out of your head. If I want to pick you up, I damn well will." I inwardly groan at the bossiness because fuck, it's attractive. And the way he just lifts me, walking as if I weigh nothing, wages a war inside my brain. I want to believe him, I want to feel comfortable in his arms, but I'm waiting for him to drop me.

It never comes.

He stops in front of the couch but doesn't sit. He just locks eyes with me, places both of his hands under my legs, and lifts me higher so my elbows can rest comfortably on his shoulders.

"I won't drop you," he whispers before his lips lightly brush against mine. Before I can apologize, he sits down, taking me with him. The moment my legs move over his hips, I feel the leverage of the cushion under my knees, and the way his cock feels against my still-covered pussy. I can't help but groan.

"That's it, baby. Feel what you do to me?" He moans as my hips move of their own accord. I start to ride him, loving the feeling of his hardness against me, and the lightning rods of pleasure it causes throughout my body. "Fuck, I always knew you'd feel amazing…" He groans again as his head falls against the back of the couch. I use that as an excuse to taste him. My lips find the crook of his neck, and when my lips tentatively kiss up the column, his intake of breath and the jerk of his hips spurs me on.

His flavor is unlike anything I imagined. I don't know why I expected him to taste like something out of a protein powder container, but he doesn't. It's intoxicating, and the longer my lips explore his skin, the more my hips ride him like I'm fucking him into the couch.

Owen's hands grip my hips, and he rocks me back and forth against his cock, sending shockwaves throughout my entire body. Before long, I feel the ripples of pleasure rumble inside as my orgasm builds, the harder I ride him. My body starts to shake, and I know I'm seconds away from coming. Owen seems to notice too, because he wraps one arm around my lower back and lifts his hips in time with each of my thrusts, his lips tracing the edge of my throat.

"Come for me, Morgan. I want to feel you fall apart in my arms." The second those words leave his mouth, I blast apart, his lips searing mine, swallowing my screams of pleasure. I can't control my rhythm as my body convulses and one of the best orgasms I've ever had rolls through me. I try not to think about how the best climax I've ever had is while I'm still fully clothed. But I'm distracted by the fact that Owen stiffens under me as my hips continue their undulations, causing another groan to leave him as he leans his head against my chest. My arms move around his neck, pulling him closer.

"Fucking hell, I haven't done that since I was a teenager," he growls against me. I lean back, laughing as his smile lights up his entire face. "God, you're so beautiful when you smile like that..." His voice lowers, and then his lips take mine in one of the sweetest kisses I have ever experienced, leaving me both sated and more confused than ever.

16

OWEN

"Why do you have that look on your face?" Matt asks from across the room as I'm jerked out of my daydream about Morgan, something that's been happening ever since she got back; it's only becoming more common the more time I spend with her.

"What are you talking about?" I say, ignoring his knowing smile as I return to looking at my emails.

"I'm talking about the look of utter happiness you've had ever since you went over to Morgan's house the other day. Care to explain?" I shake my head, ignoring him completely. "You can ignore me all you want, but I will ask you the same question every day for as long as it takes for you to tell me what happened." I sigh because I know he's not bluffing. He did the same thing when I started dating Bailey. He wanted to know why I was being so stupid, but I had no answer for him. I thought it was a good idea at the time.

"Fine, I kissed Morgan." That's an incredible understatement for what happened, but I really don't want to say that I kissed her more than three times and let her grind on my cock until we both came in our pants like teenagers making out in my parent's basement.

"Morgan? It's about fucking time," he replies as he passes me and goes to put some new flyers against the window.

"What are you talking about?"

"Come on, the minute she came home, and you saw her, I noticed the changes in you. You've been in love with her for so long. I'm just happy I don't have to hear about it anymore." I look at him, confused because I never talked to him about Morgan—at least not that I remember. "Whenever you get drunk, you talk about how much you regret letting her get away, blah blah blah. It got annoying, hence why I don't get drunk with you anymore." My eyes widen because I just thought he stopped drinking. Apparently, it was me all along. I can't help the laugh that escapes me.

S.A. CLAYTON

"Fuck, man, I thought you went dry." He chuckles and shakes his head.

"Nope, just avoiding drunk you." I throw a towel at him as I lean back against the wall. "So, what happened? Did you seal the deal?" I quirk an eyebrow and softly shake my head. "Why not? The girl looks at you like you're ice cream on a hot day." I sigh because I know that admitting any of this will lead to incessant probing, and the threat of Matt holding this over my head forever is real. "Come on, man, as much as I make fun of you, I actually do care about your life."

"Fine. No, we haven't *sealed the deal*." Just hearing the words leave my mouth makes me sick because I want nothing more than to feel her wrapped around me. But we can't. At least, not yet.

"Why not?"

"She needs to understand that I want more." His brow creases as his eyes search mine.

"More?" I chuckle at his disbelief.

"I've been waiting for this moment since I was sixteen. I can't rush it. I *won't* rush this."

"Why so cautious?"

It takes a moment to get the words together before I answer. "Because I can't lose her again. If going slowly allows her to see how much I really care about her, then I'll do it for as long as it takes for the truth to sink in."

He smiles as he heads into the back, and I hear the bell go off on the front door, letting me know that someone came in. The minute my eyes lock with the beauty crossing the threshold, I can't help the smile that overtakes my face.

"You busy?" Morgan asks as she shuts the door behind her and heads to where I'm leaning against the front counter. She looks gorgeous as always. She's wearing her workout clothes, but this time, I see a bright pink sports bra peeking out, and my mouth starts to water at the prospect of seeing more of it.

"Hey!" Morgan says, snapping her fingers in front of my face. "Eyes up here, bud." My eyes jerk to hers, only to see the best smile I've ever seen on her face.

"Come here," I say, hooking my fingers around her neck and pulling her close as my lips descend to hers. The kiss isn't x-rated, but when we hear a throat clearing behind us, we break apart as if our parents just caught us. Fuck, I could kiss her all day. Getting through training is going to be a bitch, especially knowing what she tastes like, and what she feels like riding my cock like a champion.

"I'll leave you two lovebirds to it. I'll be in the

back if you need me," Matt says before heading back to the storage room and leaving us alone once again.

"You ready to get started?" I ask, loving the blush that travels up her neck as she nods and goes and gets the mats off the wall to place them on the floor. "I was thinking we could do something different today, if you're up for it." She nods enthusiastically, but I also see the hint of fear in her eyes. I soften, cupping her face. "I would never make you do something I didn't think you could do, okay? You don't have to be worried about any of that in front of me, all right? I support you, no matter what." I give her a quick kiss before we start stretching. After a few minutes, she looks at me, sweat dripping down her forehead.

"What's the new thing you wanted to try?" She's hesitant. Most clients are when I mix things up—and that's the reason I do it. If you do something too many times, if you get too comfortable, so does your body, and you stop pushing yourself to go harder. That's why I always try to switch things up every few weeks. It makes things more interesting, and honestly, it gets better results.

"I wanted to try a circuit. I know we've been focusing on cardio and weights. A circuit is still the same thing, but this time, I'll time you." Her brows furrow, so I take out the papers in my back pocket and show her my plan.

"We have six exercises. All are either cardio or strength training-related, but the catch is that you are at each station for thirty seconds. Once you finished the first round, you have a minute's rest, then you do it all over again. We do that three times." Her eyes bulge because she knows how hard this is going to be.

"Are you fucking kidding me? That sounds awful," she sputters, and I start laughing, helping her off the floor and getting all the equipment we'll need.

"I know it sounds terrible, but I promise you'll feel so much better after you finish. And there might even be a reward in it for you if you complete it."

"Oh? Like what?" she says, quirking an eyebrow. I feel a tightness in my chest when I think about the fact that she's finally mine. I've spent the last ten years knowing that this is where I was supposed to be, and now that I'm finally here...I will not take it for granted, no matter what. I walk over to where she's standing and lean in, kissing her softly, traveling across her jaw until I stop at the shell of her ear.

"There might be an orgasm or two for you after

this...if you complete it and work your ass off." I add that last part because even though I want her to stay the way she is—because I think she's gorgeous no matter what—I know she wants to do this. And the trainer in me needs to see the results—for her. She nods her head as she starts to lean in for another kiss, but I back away. I shake my head and jerk my chin in the direction of the circuit setup. "No sugar for you until you finish." She groans and starts loosening up.

"You ready?" I ask, and she nods.

She crushed that circuit, and I made her come more times than she could count on one hand.

I think this reward system is going to work just fine.

17

MORGAN

I arrive at work early, a large coffee in my hand because I didn't get to sleep until way too late last night. Owen is a texter and loves to message me at all hours of the day—something I've learned over the past few weeks of our relationship. At least I think we're in one. We haven't had *the* conversation yet, but given the things he was texting me last night…I'm pretty sure I know the answer.

As I set my coffee on the counter, I hear a quiet knock on the front door. When I turn around, I can't stop the smile that crosses my face as Owen's gorgeous visage fills the glass.

"What are you doing here?" I ask, opening the door and letting him in, then locking it behind us once more. The store doesn't open for another few hours, but I wanted to get here and take stock of inventory before we got too busy.

"Had a client on the books early this morning, but she canceled. So, I thought I'd come over and see my girlfriend." He gives me that megawatt smile before leaning in for a kiss, but I pull away.

"Is that what I am?" I say shyly, wanting to know the answer but embarrassed for asking at the same time. Owen shakes his head and leans his forehead against mine as he takes my face in his hands and lifts my chin so I meet his eyes.

"You are way more than my girlfriend. But for now, we can start with that." He winks, sending my ovaries into overdrive. God, he's gorgeous with his blue eyes looking straight into mine as he leans down and places a light kiss on my lips.

"You know, if you keep looking at me like that, I might just have to do something about it," he says, laughing as he walks past me and picks up my coffee. He takes a sip, grimacing at the taste. "What the fuck is this?" he asks as if my drink disgusts him.

"It's a mocha latte," I state matter-of-factly as I take the cup from his hands, taking a sip and moaning in the most exaggerated way possible. But when I set the cup back down and meet his eyes, he's not laughing. His eyes bore into mine, burning with the fire I've come to expect from him.

"What?" I ask, looking around and making sure nothing's wrong. He just shakes his head and cups the side of my face as he leans in and kisses me.

"Those sounds you just made are making it really hard for me not to take you right here on this counter." I moan at the image of what that would look like. For a second, I wonder if it's possible. "Fuck, baby, you are driving me crazy," he mutters against my lips as he kisses me with everything he has. He pushes me against the counter before lifting me so I'm sitting with him between my legs.

"Owen, we can't do this here..." I say as my head tips back, giving his lips access to my neck as he trails kisses down the center of my chest and over the swell of my breasts. "Becca is going to be here any minute," I say, but it seems to go in one ear and out the other. Owen continues his assault on my senses as his hands grab my ass and he pulls me closer, leaving not even an inch of space between us.

"I don't care. *Fuck, baby*, you feel like magic against me." His lips find mine once more, and for the millionth time over the past few weeks, I wonder why he's waiting to go all the way. We have done everything else, yet the minute I mention sex, he tells me he wants to show me that this is more than just another fuck for him. At first, I loved him for it. I thought it was sweet that he wanted to make sure I knew he liked me for me and not for the service I could provide. But after the second week of us being officially "together", I started getting frustrated. And now, going into week three, I'm downright pissed.

"No!" I say, pushing him away. "You are not doing this to me again. You are not getting me all hot and bothered only to get me off and then run away. Not happening." I jump off the counter and head to the front door, opening it.

"Come on, baby, you know why I want to wait," he says, making his way over to me and lightly kissing my cheek. "Trust me when I say it's almost impossible for me to walk away from you and not sink into that sweet heat I know you have between your legs. I've spent over a decade dreaming about what it would feel like. But I want to make sure we're both ready for that step, okay?" Damn him and his sweet words. I nod sadly, but he lifts my chin and smiles down at me as if I'm the eighth wonder of the world. "I'll see you tonight. Okay? When you're done, come to the gym. We can work out a bit, all right?" I nod as he kisses me lightly and then heads over to the gym.

Just as I'm about to close the door, I hear Becca calling from down the street. I wave her in.

"Thanks! Was that Owen I just saw leaving?" she asks as I nod. She stops in the middle of the room, looking around.

"What?" I ask, confused at what she's doing.

"I'm just wondering what I need to disinfect since you clearly had a quickie before work." My intake of breath sends her into a fit of laughter. "I'm kidding...obviously. Unless it's true. In that case, please tell which surfaces I need to clean before we open." She starts laughing again as I roll my eyes and go back to inventory.

Today is going to be a long day.

* * *

"Mom?" I ask, walking around the counter and hugging her. "What are you doing here?"

"Can't a mother come to see her daughter?" She smiles, looking around at the store. "Plus, you've been so busy here, your father and I haven't seen you in too long." Guilt floods me at the reality of what she just said. Making sure the store had a successful opening meant that spending less time at home. Therefore, less time with my parents.

"I'm sorry, Mom. I'll be sure to come by this weekend for dinner," I say, hoping what I say next doesn't send her into a fit. "Do you mind if I bring the guy I've been seeing? I'd love for you guys to meet him." I purposefully don't mention the man I'm talking about his Owen because I know what that conversation will entail.

"Sure! That would be lovely! I didn't know you were seeing someone…" Her voice is almost sad, and I know she thinks I've been keeping it from her. On the one hand, I have, but it's only because I know how much she hates him for what he did to me in high school.

"It's fairly new, just a few weeks." She raises an eyebrow, and I roll my eyes. "I wanted to make sure it was the real deal before introducing him to you and Daddy." She gives me a smile that tells me she understands.

"Sweetie, it's all right. I didn't introduce your father to Grandad until at least six months in." My eyes widen, because knowing what Grandad is like, he couldn't have been happy. "So, who is this young man that's stolen your heart so fast?"

I take a deep breath. I wanted to wait, but I can't lie to her. "Owen," I say as fast as I can. From the blank expression on her face, I know she doesn't believe me.

"Please tell me you don't mean the same Owen who broke your heart," she says, sadness radiating off her in waves.

"Mom, I know that what he did back then was bad, but we've talked about it. If you just give him a chance, I think you'll come to like him again." She gives me a skeptical look before her shoulders slump, and she brings me in for another hug.

"Does he make you happy?" she asks. I nod my head, hugging her back even tighter. "Then that's enough for me. Bring him over for dinner. I'll warn your father, but I can't promise he'll be as understanding as I am." I chuckle as I nod, knowing that I may be leading Owen to the slaughter.

I hope he'll forgive me.

18

OWEN

"Why did I think this was a good idea?" Morgan admits as we sit in my truck in front of her parents' house.

"Hey," I say, forcing her to look at me. Her eyes are scared, her teeth worrying her lower lip to the point where I have to actively stop looking at her so I don't just kiss the hell out of her right here. "It's going to be okay, I promise." I kiss her lightly before opening my door and heading around the front of my truck to open hers.

"Such a gentleman," she teases as I help her out and kiss her one last time, hidden behind the truck's cab.

"I'm not always a gentleman." I groan against her

lips as she kisses me harder, pulling me closer as her hands clasp my face.

"I don't want what happens in there to affect what happens out here..." I know she's worried. I've seen it in her eyes the last couple of days. I didn't think I needed to reassure her, but apparently, I was wrong.

"Baby, listen to me. There is nothing they can say that will make me stop the feelings I have for you, okay? I know they hate me for what I did to you, and they have every right to, but I'm here so they can see how much I care for you. How much I want to make up for all those lost years because of my teenage delusions of grandeur." She gives me a small smile before I kiss her lightly one last time and take her hand, leading us to the front door.

"I just want you to be prepared," she murmurs the closer we get to the front steps. I squeeze her hand silently, and before I have a chance to repeat my stance again that nothing will change the way I feel about her, the front door opens. A very large, imposing man steps out.

"Hey, pumpkin," Mr. Lawson says with a big smile on his face. For a split second, I wonder if Morgan was overreacting. Maybe they've forgiven me for what I did all those years ago. But then the man's eyes turn to me. "Owen," he states. No *hello*, no smile. Just a stern look that tells me loud and clear that tonight is going to be anything but easy.

"Daddy..." Morgan warns as Mr. Lawson's eyes shift from mine to his daughter's.

"What?" he questions, a big smile crossing his face as he starts laughing, holding out his hand to me. "Sorry, son, I was only joking. It's nice to see you again." Morgan swats at her father's arm as I stand there dumbfounded.

"Seriously, Dad? That was not funny," Morgan says as her eyes flick to mine. I know my brow is still furrowed. "You okay?" she asks, and for a second, I think she's talking to her father. When no one answers, I shake myself out of whatever haze I'm in and nod.

"Nice to see you again, Mr. Lawson," I state, still not really knowing where I stand but happy the stern look has disappeared at least.

"Please, call me James." He gives my hand a shake and pulls me in for a quick hug that sets every limb at ease. I glance over at Morgan. She just rolls her eyes at the stunt her father just pulled.

"Come on, Owen, let's go inside." I follow her into the modest bungalow that looks identical to its neighbors from the outside. But the minute I step foot into the house, it's like I've been transported to high school. The décor hasn't changed a bit since the last time I was here. Every wall is covered in wallpaper, every piece of furniture some kind of floral pattern, and the pink shag carpet under my feet pulls the entire look together.

"Mom! We're here!" Morgan yells from the doorway. The second her mother pokes her head out of the kitchen and locks eyes with me, I know her stern look isn't a joke. Diana Lawson is the one I will have to win over.

"Honey! So glad you're here," she says, wiping her hands on a tea towel and walking out and our way. She envelops Morgan in a hug and then turns to me. "Owen, it's nice to see you." She isn't unwelcoming exactly, but her tone tells me everything I need to know.

"It's nice to see you, too, Mrs. Lawson. I appreciate your hospitality." Her eyes narrow, and I can see her brain working to find a way to twist what I just said into something she can hold against me later. Morgan interrupts her by taking my hand and leading me into the living room.

"You watching the game, Dad?" James nods as he sits down in his lounge chair, the same seat that

Morgan used to sit in when we studied together. He turns up the volume. We take the hint and sit down on the couch as Diana goes back into the kitchen to finish dinner.

"I'll be right back," I say to Morgan, who is just as engrossed in the game as her father. I make my way into the kitchen. When I poke my head in through the door, I take a second to admire the way Mrs. Lawson commands the kitchen. Every burner has something cooking, and the oven is on and full of something that smells delicious.

"Mrs. Lawson?" I call, hoping not to startle her. "Do you mind if I help?" I'm horrible in the kitchen since my mother kicked me out for burning French toast. But I know this is the only way I'm going to get through to the woman who hates me right now.

"Oh no, dear. That's fine. I have everything under control." She dismisses me faster than I thought she would, but I still don't move. "Owen, you don't need to suck up to me," she states matter-of-factly, and I can't help but smile because that bluntness has definitely been passed down to her daughter.

"That's not what this is about. I know you're still upset about what happened all those years ago, and I just want to explain myself." I told Morgan I was going to do this last night. She told me I didn't have to, but I know it's the right thing to do. If I don't explain, they'll hate me like I've hated myself for years.

"The only person you owe an explanation to is my daughter. And since she's forgiven you, I guess I should, as well." I shake my head. That's not good enough for me because I know those seeds of doubt will fester unless she knows the whole story.

"With all due respect, I believe I owe you and your husband the truth." So, I sit at their kitchen table and explain everything. From my feelings for Morgan, to Kelly using them as a way to separate us, and everything in between. By the end, Diana is in tears.

"Oh, my sweet boy. The fact that you did all of that to protect my daughter from someone willing to do her harm shows exactly the kind of man you are." She gets up out of her chair and opens her arms. "Come here," she says. I smile, getting up and hugging her the best I can since she's half my size. "I don't agree with what you did. I still think you should have talked to her instead of ignoring her, but I understand you were in a bad position." I nod my head as we break apart.

"I've loved your daughter for so long, and I've carried the guilt from that day with me all these years—until she forgave me just a few weeks ago. I need you to know that I will never do anything like that to her again. I promise." She shakes her head, a small smile playing at the edges of her lips.

"As much as I appreciate you saying that, you shouldn't make promises you can't keep, Owen." Her eyes are stern, but I know it's not with ill intent.

"But I can keep this one. Hurting Morgan, it hurts me. And in the end, she is everything. I want to protect that." She gives me a slight nod and a smile, shooing me out of the kitchen and back into the living room.

"Where did you go?" Morgan asks from the couch, her eyes still glued to the television. I take my hand and cup the side of her face, bringing her eyes to meet mine. When they do, I can't help but lean in and kiss her lightly.

"I just had a talk with your mom." She goes to say something, but I shake my head. "Baby, it's fine. We talked. I explained everything, and it's all good." She quirks an eyebrow, and I smile. "Promise." I kiss her one last time, this time breaking apart only when her dad yells something at the TV and I remember where we are.

"Thank you," she whispers as I pull her against my chest and hold her close.

"Anything for you," I say, kissing the top of her head. From the corner of my eye, I see her father look my way. When our eyes meet, he gives me a slight nod of his head.

For the first time all day, I breathe a sigh of relief.

19

MORGAN

"So, am I invited to this birthday bash of yours?" Owen murmurs against my neck as we hide in the storage room. Becca is watching the store, and since I've managed to hire a few part-time workers that have been great, I know everything's fine. It gives me more time to spend with my family, and I've gotten into a routine of working out with Owen in the morning and then going home for breakfast and a shower before heading in to close. There are a few days here and there where I hate everything about the routine, especially when Owen decides I've become too complacent and switches up our workouts. I'm always exhausted the next day.

"I could be persuaded to invite you. For a

price..." I whisper against the shell of his ear, wanting nothing more than to strip him down and have my way with him right here. But no matter how much I beg, he always stops me before we go too far. Honestly, I'm still a little pissed.

"And what would that be?" he asks, kissing my neck, making me weak in the knees. I pull his face back to mine, his hands gripping my hips so hard I know I'll see finger marks there later.

"You know what I want," I whisper, my lips tracing the edges of his, knowing what we both want. But he's still holding back, and I need to understand why.

"Baby, you have no idea how much I want to give that to you..." He groans, his forehead leaning against mine as he takes a deep breath. Frustration boils out of me as I push him away, running my fingers through my hair. "Morgan..." He groans again, his hands in the pockets of his jeans.

"Don't you dare say whatever was about to come out of your mouth. I never thought that I would have to beg my boyfriend to sleep with me. Do you know how embarrassing that is? Do you know how it makes me feel?" Emotions start to well up, and I silently curse the tears that threaten to surface.

"M, you have to know how much I want you..."

he says, wrapping his arms around me from behind and resting his chin on my shoulder. "You are the sexiest, hottest woman I have ever seen. Period. I get hard just watching you. Just *thinking* about you. I go to bed at night dreaming of what it would be like to have you wrapped around me, to feel your warmth surrounding me." I moan at the images he projects as his hands roam over my stomach. The second I realize where his hands are, I lock up. Being naked in front of a man isn't something that is new to me—it's not even something that scares me most of the time—but with Owen, the idea of him seeing what I see as my flaws scares the crap out of me. No matter how much I want him, there is always that small voice in the back of my head telling me that he might be disgusted once he sees all of me.

"Morgan, I'm not waiting for your benefit. I'm doing it for mine." I shake my head because that seems like a lie. "It's true. I've waited for you for over ten years. I don't want to rush this... I want you to fully understand how I feel about you before we take that next step."

"I do understand." He shakes his head.

"No, you don't. And the fact that you still lock up when I touch you here,"—his fingers flex against my stomach—"tells me I'm right." I eye him suspiciously, and when I go to say something, he kisses me softly. "M, you're my girlfriend, hell you're more than that, okay? I don't think there are words big enough to describe how much you mean to me." I nod my head, turning so I can see his eyes. When they meet mine, I can't help but melt. No matter how frustrated I get with his plan, the man knows how to use his words.

"Fine, but just know that if we don't have sex before my birthday, I will make your life a living hell." He chuckles, taking my face in his hands and kissing me.

"Deal." He winks but steps forward, backing me up against the wall. "So, am I invited to your birthday party?" he whispers against the shell of my ear.

"Do you want to come?" I can't help the nervousness that comes with the invitation. He knows what happened with Aaron. He knows what my ex did and how much it hurt. And the idea of exposing myself in that way again creates this pit in my stomach that I thought I filled a long time ago.

It takes Owen a second, but his eyes soften, his hand coming up to cup my cheek once more in a way that makes me weak in the knees. His lips brush mine ever so gently before he whispers, "I wouldn't miss it for the world."

* * *

"How was your flight?" I ask Ben as Allie looks around the store, checking out all the new inventory.

"Long. We came from visiting my family in London. We haven't really slept since we left for the airport, and that was,"—he looks at his watch—"forty-eight hours ago." My eyes bulge, knowing how Allie gets when she doesn't get enough sleep.

"Shit. Well, what the hell are you guys doing here, then? Shouldn't you be crashing at the hotel I told you not to stay at?" Ben gives that smile he's known for, and for the thousandth time since I first met him, I thank God that Allie found him—his accent doesn't hurt either.

"As much as we appreciate the gesture, we like our privacy," he says with a wink just as Allie rounds the corner and gives him the eye.

"You guys talking about me?" she teases, leaning into Ben's embrace. I smile as he kisses the top of her head. "So," she says, looking at me, "when are we going shopping?" She can't be serious.

"Aren't you tired?" I ask, looking at Ben, who looks like he might fall over at any second. She just shakes her head, looking up at Ben and realizing that he might be dead on his feet. "On second thought, maybe we should do that tomorrow." I nod my head, and Ben shakes his.

"Allie honey, go. I'll head back to the hotel and rest." She eyes him with a concerned gaze, and he just bends to kiss her lightly. They share some whispered words as I head back out to the floor and check to make sure Becca is good for the night.

"You good? I'm going out with Allie. I have my cell if you need anything." Becca gives me that *I know, Mom* look, and I smile. "Okay," I say, holding up my hands. "Just don't burn the place down," I joke.

"Don't worry, I have like three other things on my to-do list before that happens." I shake my head, both loving her and annoyed by her at the same time.

"Funny. Just call if anything happens, okay?" She nods as Allie comes out of the back, Ben following not far behind.

"Let's go!" Allie squeals, leaving Ben's hand behind and taking mine instead. "Bye, Ben!" she says as we leave the store and head down the boardwalk.

"So, where are we going?" she asks as I bask in the feel of the sunshine on my face. I've spent so much time inside the store or inside Owen's gym that I keep forgetting there's a thing called daylight.

"Well, I had this idea..." My heart starts beating because I've been planning this for a few days, and I know it can either go very, very well—or incredibly badly.

"I'm listening," Allie says, taking my arm as I lead us to the end of the street. When we stop in front of the store, her eyes light up. When I tell her my plan, her eyes light up even more, and a sneaky smile crosses her face. "Girl, you are in for a world of trouble when you get home." I wink, opening the door and walking in.

I'm surrounded by lace, colors, textures, and shapes, and when I wipe my hands on the leg of my jeans, the nerves start to set in.

"Calm down, it's just lingerie," Allie mutters as she takes my hand and leads me to the back of the store where I can tell they keep the more out-there sets. "If you're so nervous, why did you want to do this?" she asks as I flip through a see-through black number that comes with a garter belt and panties with a gaping hole in them.

Nope. Not for me.

"Owen won't give in. I've tried everything, including begging for sex, but he keeps saying he wants me to know that he likes me for more than just that." Allie eyes me, and I can't help when mine roll into the back of my head. "I know, it makes him even more perfect. But when a girl is this frustrated, she'll do almost anything…" I keep the fact that it's been almost a year since a man has even come close to having sex with me to myself. Honestly, the idea of Owen doing just that has been a feature in my spank bank for the past few weeks, but I want the real thing. I *need* the real thing before I go insane.

"Here." Allie hands me a few outfits and points to the changing room. "Try them on, take a picture, and send them to him. I guarantee the minute he gets them, he won't be saying no to you for much longer." Her eyebrows rise and fall, and I laugh as I head into the room and finally look at what she handed me.

The red one is a simple baby doll top with a thong that leaves very little to the imagination. Then there's the purple one-piece that is modest but very sexy in its own right. But the moment I see the white set, I know it's the one. I pull out my phone and text Owen.

Me: *Is there anything I can say to make you change your mind about the sex stuff?*

It's to the point, and I know he might take it the

wrong way. I'm hoping he answers the way I expect, because that's the only way this is going to work.

Owen: *Were you thinking of persuading me?*

He's teasing, and I can't help the smile.

Me: *I was thinking of getting something nice to wear tonight for when you come over.*

I change into the white number, look at myself in the mirror, and wonder for the seven-thousandth time today what the hell I'm doing. I don't do this. I don't wear skimpy lingerie. I don't expose myself this way to anyone, let alone the guy I've been pining for since I was sixteen. When I look in the mirror, I expect to see my imperfections. I anticipate my eyes falling to my stomach. I imagine my fingers pulling at the fabric, making it so it's easier to cover more of my body. But what actually happens makes my breath hitch, and my hands start to tremble. Because what I notice in the mirror isn't the fat girl that every guy before wanted me to see. What I see is the curvy woman Owen's hands grab for every time we're in the same room together. I notice a woman who isn't a size two but looks damn good in white lace. And then I realize in that moment that no matter how much weight I lose, no matter what size my jeans' tag says, at the end of the day, Owen likes the Morgan Lawson that's staring back at me in the mirror.

And that's enough.

For now.

When Owen sends back a heart emoji, I take one last look at myself in the mirror and do something I swore I would never do. I open up my camera, snap a picture, and try not to overthink it. Instead, I send it to Owen before I change my mind.

I redress in my work clothes and head out into the store where Allie is waiting. When she sees that I'm still carrying the white lace, she gives me a knowing look.

"I knew you'd pick that one. He's going to go insane when he sees you." She winks as we stand in line to pay. When my phone vibrates in my hand, I glance down to see what Owen said. When I do, I almost drop my phone.

Owen: *You have no idea what you just started.*

20

OWEN

*F*uck me.

The second that picture comes through on my phone, I know I'm a dead man. How the hell am I supposed to resist her when she looks like a goddess in white lace? Thank God I'm standing behind the front desk because the erection I'm sporting would definitely turn some heads, and the only head I want to turn is currently buying lingerie that hugs every amazing curve of her body.

I've dreamt about what Morgan would look like dripping in lace, lying on my bed and throwing her head back in ecstasy. And from the way my body reacted to seeing that photo? God knows I won't have a chance in hell of resisting her much longer.

"Incoming," Matt whispers as my eyes move in the direction of the front door, only to see Bailey strolling in as if she owns the place.

"Fuck..." I mutter, placing my phone beside the computer, rounding the counter and cutting her off before she can get too far.

"What are you doing here, Bailey?" Her eyes go wide as if she's surprised that I'm agitated by the fact that she's here yet again, even though I've asked her repeatedly to stay away.

"I wanted to work out," she says, giving me a coy smile as she plays with a loose strand of her hair. That move used to make me fall to my knees. But now? Now, I just want her to leave me the fuck alone.

"Really? In jeans and a halter top?" I question, knowing full well that's not why she's here. "Come on, Bailey, just tell me what you want so I can get back to work." *Or better yet, go find Morgan and sample that lingerie for myself.*

"Can't a girl come and watch some hot guys work out?" She eyes Matt, who just rolls his eyes and goes back to training. Bailey doesn't take her eyes off Matt as I shake my head and walk back to the front counter. I know she thinks she's making me jealous, but honestly, it's laughable that Matt would want anything to do with her.

"Owen, I need you for a sec!" Matt calls from across the room. I take a deep breath and pass Bailey, who hooks her fingers around my arm, stopping me in my tracks.

"Owen, please. I just want to talk." Nope. Not interested.

"Don't be afraid to let yourself out while I'm gone," I mutter, taking her hand and lifting it off my arm as I walk away. I hope she takes the hint.

The second I get to within inches of where Matt is standing, he whispers, "Just thought you could use an out." I look back at Bailey, who leans against the front counter, looking directly at me, her bottom lip caught between her teeth.

"Thanks, man. I'm going to the back for a bit. Organize some shit in the office. Let me know when she's gone and it's safe to return." He slaps me on the back, squeezing my shoulder for good measure.

"I told you a year ago she was a bad idea." He did, and I was too preoccupied by the fact that she was hot and willing, something that, at the time, was the most important thing to me. But now? Now, I want more.

"Shut up." I laugh as I head back into the office,

checking over my shoulder one last time and seeing Bailey leaning in the same spot, her eyes following my every move.

I'M JUST PULLING up to Morgan's driveway as her front door opens. I watch as she leans against the doorjamb. She's wearing a simple black dress that hugs every curve, and with her blond hair down in waves framing that gorgeous face, she looks like an angel.

"Hey there, stranger," Morgan says as I walk up the front steps of her house and stop an inch from where she's standing. Her head tilts back, her eyes meet mine, and what I see staring back at me is a look I've never seen before. At least, not from Morgan. She kisses me lightly on the lips as she turns away and walks back into the house. I know she wants me to follow her, but all I can do is stand there and watch her walk away. Because the roll of her hips, the way her head turns as she beckons me inside, tells me I'm in big trouble.

"M, you look gorgeous," I mutter, walking up behind her and grabbing her hips, hauling her against me. The moment my fingers inch their way past her hips and down the sides of her thighs, I feel it—the unmistakable ridge of that lingerie. I groan. "Are you wearing what I think you are?" I whisper against the skin of her neck, loving the shiver that goes through her as my lips trail up, stopping at the shell of her ear. "Because I've been thinking about that picture all day, baby, and my control is wearing thin." She leans her head against my chest as my fingers dig into her thighs, inching up her dress, exposing the garter belt and the top of her stockings. Fuck me, she's a sight to behold.

"What if I don't want you to be in control?" She groans as her hands find mine and she pushes them lower, under the fabric of her dress, against her bare skin. The confidence in her touch, the way her body moves against mine is fucking sexy as hell, and when my fingers find the edge of her panties, she sags against me.

"Fuck, M, you are driving me crazy." She says nothing as her ass grinds against my now rock-hard cock that strains against the front of my jeans. The heat coming off her pussy is intoxicating as I find her clit and gently tease it over the fabric. "Are you sure you're ready?" I ask quietly, watching her eyes close as her hand grabs mine and keeps it against her heat. I can feel how wet she is and know the answer before she even says a word.

"Yes…" She groans, using my fingers for her pleasure as I simply stand there and just watch. Her fingers dig into my hand as she starts to grind against me, getting closer and closer to the orgasm I know she wants. But before she can, I pull away and turn her to face me.

"I need you to be totally sure," I say, taking her face in my hands and sealing my lips to hers. It doesn't take much for the kiss to get out of hand, but this time, Morgan's the one that backs away.

"You want to know if I'm sure?" she asks, and I stand there motionless, nodding my head as she reaches behind her and pulls the zipper of her dress down her back past the curve of her ass. I watch it fall to the floor.

I can't describe the sound that escapes my lips as I take in the white lace bra that barely covers her breasts. My mouth salivates at the sight of the mounds spilling out over the edge of the cups, just waiting for my lips. Then my eyes travel south, over the curve of her stomach, landing on the strip of fabric covering her pussy, and the garter belt that barely holds up the sheer tights surrounding her thighs. She looks like a goddamn pinup girl. There isn't a man on Earth that could stand where I am and not sink to his knees at the sight. She looks like a sex goddess. She looks like every fantasy I've ever had come to life, and for the first time in weeks, I realize that she's mine. Right here, right now, she's giving herself to me. And, fuck me, I'm ready to take her.

21

MORGAN

*O*wen's eyes never leave me as I walk toward him, my hips swaying in a way that I know accentuates my curves, allowing him to see every inch of what I have on display. My heart beats so fast and so strong that I swear if he gets close enough, he'll hear it. As his eyes drink me in, I wait for the inevitable. I wait for the nervous feeling to settle in my stomach; for the fear to paste itself over my skin and stay there, ruining the moment. But I feel nothing. All I feel are the butterflies in my stomach at the prospect of his hands on my skin. All I can focus on are his eyes as they cascade over every inch of my body, his hands fisting at his sides the closer I get, almost as if he's waiting for me to make the first move.

"Owen?" I say breathlessly. His eyes flick to mine, and I suck in a breath at the pure devotion I see staring back at me. He doesn't say a word as I stop in front of him, my head tilting back to keep his eyes on mine. I reach out, taking one of his hands and slowly bringing it to my stomach. This is my biggest fear. My biggest struggle is that I have never—and probably will never—have a flat stomach. But when I close my eyes, feeling his fingers lightly brushing against the soft skin of my midsection as his fingers curve around my waist, tugging me closer, everything I thought I would be worried about falls away. I simply bask in his touch.

"Morgan, baby. You are..." He doesn't finish the sentence because my lips fuse to his. I swallow the groan that leaves his throat as I pull myself flush against him. Our teeth clash as his hands grasp me under the ass and he lifts me. I wrap my legs around his waist. "Bedroom..." he groans, kissing down the column of my neck, sending little shockwaves of pleasure throughout my entire body. I point down the hall, and before I can say a word, he leads us both into my bedroom, depositing me on the bed and staring down at me from hooded eyes.

"Owen, what are you—?" I start, but he holds up

his hands and stops me. My heart races as he lowers himself to the floor, his fingers dancing over the exposed skin above my thighs as he delicately and ever so slowly undoes every single clasp of my garter belt. He leans down, lightly kissing my thigh as he slowly lowers the stockings past my knees, nipping at every exposed piece of skin along the way. My hips lift, wetness pooling as he does the same to the other leg, sending my head back against the mattress, and my eyes rolling to the back of my head in pleasure.

"You have no idea how amazing you look right now," he whispers, kissing up my stomach, past my breasts, and stopping just before my lips. His fingers find the edge of my panties once more, and I groan, loving the feeling of his skin against mine. "You. Are. Perfect," he says between kisses as his fingers delve into my heat, causing my breath to hitch, and my back to bow off the bed. As much as I love the feeling of his fingers inside me, that's not what I want right now. My hands make their way into his hair, grasping the loose strands and pulling him closer, my lips attacking him as my hips grind against his hand.

"Owen, please..." I beg, hoping he gets that I need

more—so much more. And from the light chuckle he emits, I know he understands. Before I can react, he pulls away, his fingers leaving my heat as he stands, staring down at me. He gives me that cocky smirk of his that sends a new wave of heat straight to my core as he pulls his shirt over his head, dropping it to the floor beside him.

Fuck. He's so freaking gorgeous, it's not fair. It's like I'm looking at a whole firefighters' calendar all wrapped up in one amazing guy. Before I think better of it, I sit up, my fingers trailing over his abs, moving past his hips to land on his jeans' waistband. My eyes move up, silently asking for permission. When he nods his head, I quickly undo his jeans, watching them fall to the floor as his cock springs free, causing my breath to catch. Commando. I don't know why that's so hot, but it is.

"You keep staring at it like that, and I won't be responsible for what happens next." His answering growl sends a shiver of anticipation through me as my eyes once more meet his, my fingers gently brushing the sides of his shaft. "Jesus, baby. Your touch feels so fucking good." I smile as I become bolder, leaning forward to kiss the tip, loving how his knees buckle in response. But it's not until my mouth closes over his cock, and his fingers delve into my hair that everything changes. The air in the room becomes thick with lust as I suck him deeper and deeper until he hits the back of my throat. I moan around his cock, loving the way it feels and tastes. But before I have a chance to do more, he pulls me off, lifting me and placing me in the middle of the bed. He wastes no time ripping my panties from my body as he shucks his jeans from around his ankles and comes over to me.

"You still okay?" he asks, kissing down my neck, settling between my breasts. His fingers find the clasp of my bra, and without hesitation, the garment comes loose. He tosses it away along with the rest of our clothes.

"Owen, please don't make me beg." He chuckles against my skin as I hear a foil wrapper being torn open, and my heart starts to race. I've dreamt about this moment for ten years, twelve if you count the years before everything went sideways.

"God, I've been waiting for this for so long." His eyes meet mine, and for a second, everything stops. The desperate feeling evaporates, and I'm left in a moment of clarity. Before I think better of it, I reach up and cup his face, bringing his eyes back to mine.

"What's wrong?" he whispers, kissing my forehead. I give him a grateful smile, knowing that what I'm about to say is right.

"I love you, Owen." No hesitation. The man in front of me has never wavered for a single moment. He makes me feel as if I matter; as if being myself is enough. And for that alone, I love him.

"Morgan?" His eyes search mine, waiting for the denial that he seems sure will come. But it doesn't. "You love me?" As if the idea of me loving him is in some way impossible, when in fact, it's the only thing I know for certain.

I nod my head, tears streaming down my face now as he gives me a full smile that takes over his entire face and steals my breath. "I think I've loved you for twelve years," I admit, hoping that admission doesn't scare him away.

"Fuck, Morgan. You have no idea how amazing it is to hear you say that…" His head lowers, his lips seeking mine as he begins to kiss me frantically. "I love you, too," he says against my lips as he pulls away and looks into my eyes that are now full of tears. "You have always been my endgame. Even when I fucked up. Even when you hated me. I never stopped hoping that you'd come back to me someday."

I can't take anymore as I pull his face to mine. Our lips dance as he stills over me, his cock pressed to my entrance. All I can think about is the way he feels against me. All I can see are his eyes as he braces himself, slowly sinking into my heat. My eyes roll into the back of my head at the sensation. This is unlike anything I have ever experienced before. The feel of him inside me is a pleasure I never thought to experience, and blows every other experience out of the water.

"Fuck, baby, you are so tight..." He moans, his forehead against mine, and his breath cascading over my lips. My hips lift of their own accord, swallowing even more of him as he sinks deeper and deeper with every passing second.

"More," I groan, wrapping my arms around his neck and pulling his lips back to mine as he bottoms out inside me. For a second, neither of us moves, we stay like that, pressed together in the most intimate way possible, just staring at each other. But then Owen starts to move and that's when everything goes into hyperdrive. The feel of him slowly fucking me has my back bowing off the bed, my fingers digging into the skin of his back, and my eyes rolling into the back of my head.

"Fuck, yes," Owen groans as he speeds up the

pace, fucking me like I've dreamed about for the past few weeks. His fingers dig into my hips as he kisses my neck, sucking on the skin and sending shock-waves directly to my clit. But it's not until his fingers find purchase against my sensitive nub that every-thing starts to unravel. The orgasm hits me hard and fast as I scream his name. He pistons even harder. It takes a few more strokes before Owen stills on top of me, his body locking as my legs wrap around his waist, loving the feel of him pulsing inside of me.

"Jesus…" he groans, his orgasm still sending shockwaves throughout his body that I can actually feel, making me chuckle underneath him. "That was…" he mutters, and I nod my head because right now there are no words for what just happened.

I moan as Owen slowly slips out of me, and I instantly miss his warmth. I watch as he takes off the condom and throws it into the trashcan beside the bed. As he gets back into bed, wrapping me in his arms and kissing the top of my head, I expect the nervousness to return, that feeling of the unknown settling over my skin once more. But it never comes.

"You know I meant every word," he says against my temple as I wrap my arm around his waist and tilt my eyes to meet his. "I do love you. So much." I smile as he lowers his lips to mine, gently kissing me.

"I love you, too," I murmur against his skin as he pulls the covers over us and tugs me even closer.

Yup, this is what happiness is supposed to feel like.

22

OWEN

She looks perfect sleeping next to me, a sheet covering the lower half of her body, the rest of her pressed directly against my chest. The sensation of her breasts against me every time she takes a breath sends arousal straight to my cock, but I know she needs her rest. I woke her way too many times last night. I needed to feel her against me, surrounding me. Tried to savor the moment because it didn't seem real.

I lean down, kissing Morgan lightly on her head as I hear the vibration of my phone from across the room. She stirs, pulling me closer. I smile, leaning my head back on the pillow, knowing life can't possibly get better than this. The vibration comes again—and again and again—to the point where I know if I don't get up, it will wake her, and I can't have that. So, I gently peel myself from her grasp, giving her my pillow to hug as I cross the room and find my cell in the back pocket of my jeans that lay discarded on the floor.

Before I look at the screen, I take one last look at Morgan as she sleeps soundly, and then look to see which bastard is blowing up my phone. The second I see the messages, my heart plummets.

Bailey.

Bailey: *Meet me at my place by noon. If not, I will send this to every person in this town.*

I scroll down to see the pictures Morgan sent me from that changing room yesterday. The ones that were the catalyst for everything that happened last night. The images I still have on my phone.

How the fuck did she get into my phone?

I shake the thought out of my head and gather my clothes off the floor to get dressed. As much as I want to stay right here and bask in every single inch of Morgan and that sweet body of hers, I know I need to fix this. I will not be the cause of more problems for her. I will not let my past and my stupid decisions be the reason for her pain, I did that enough when we were teenagers.

I make my way across the room, sitting on the

edge of the bed and just stare at her. The woman who I'd give everything up for, the person who has quickly become as essential as breathing. And in that moment, I know I will do whatever it takes to protect her from Bailey. Including lying to her.

I don't plan to wake her up, but I can't help the impulse as my fingers trace the line of her jaw, following the curve of her neck and down the center if her back. Her skin is so fucking soft, and I can't help the low moan that escapes my throat at the feel of her under my fingers.

"If you're going to tease me, then you'd better get undressed." A chuckle escapes me as the weight of my cell phone presses against my leg, reminding me of what I still have to do.

"Sorry, gorgeous, but I've gotta go." Her head lifts, eyes meeting mine as the guilt starts to rise within me. I'm not naïve to the fact that without me, this wouldn't be happening until I took her again and again in the morning light. Instead, I'm leaving her naked, looking beautiful as the sunlight shines on her face.

"Leave? But it's only…" She looks over at her clock and sees that it's after nine. "Wow, I haven't slept this late since college." We both laugh as I brush the hair out of her eyes. She turns, taking the sheets with her, covering her chest. "Why do you have to leave?" God, the uncertainty in her eyes cuts me deep, but I lean forward and kiss her with everything I have, needing to show her without words what I can't say right now. That no matter what happens, what happened last night was real, and that I love her no matter what.

"I just need to deal with something at the gym. I'll be back before you know it." I wink, giving her my best smile as I kiss her one last time, hoping whatever Bailey has planned doesn't touch her.

EVERYTHING around me reminds me that I left Morgan alone, when all I want to do is be with her. Stay with her. But right now, I need to protect her in the only way I can, and that's by keeping her out of this entirely.

Driving clears my head, always has. So, for the past few hours, I've simply driven around aimlessly, trying to think up a scenario where everyone wins, where there's no drama. But I come up empty. The entire time, I tried to figure out how this could have happened at all. How the fuck did Bailey get those pictures? How am I going to convince her to delete them? And how am I going to get Morgan to forgive me? Because I'm not naïve enough to think I'll get out of this unscathed.

"Fuck…" I mutter as a very familiar figure leans against the column of my front porch. Bailey looks like she always does in her tight short-shorts and tube top with her long, blond hair up in her signature ponytail. My eyes close as I lean my head back against the seat of the car, basking in the silence that I know will evaporate the second I get out.

"Come on, Owen, get out here," Bailey says while tapping on my window, scaring the crap out of me. I look over, only to watch her arms cross over her chest, her hip jutting out as her foot starts tapping on the asphalt.

"Why are you here, anyway? I thought I was going to meet you at your place," I mutter as I get out of the car and smirk at her sharp intake of breath as I push past her.

"I wanted to make sure I saw you." I look back, rolling my eyes at the look of desire on her face, knowing she's using this as a ploy to get me away from Morgan. And right now, it's working. And I hate it.

"Well, you're here, so let's get this over with." I open the front door, leaving it open as I head through the narrow hallway and into my kitchen. I want to be far away from any soft surfaces, because I know Bailey, and I know she will use whatever she can to get me to cave to her demands—and that includes her body.

"You know, for someone who claimed to love me not even two months ago, you're being a real dick." I can't help the laugh that bursts from my chest because she can't be serious. But when I meet her gaze, I realize she believes every word she just said.

I shake my head, going to the fridge and getting a beer. "You know, for someone who claims to still love me, you have a fucked-up way of showing it." I take a swig of my beer, knowing its barely past morning but I need something to get me through this nightmare. As she saunters over and stands in front of me, her bottom lip between her teeth and her fingers playing with the hem of her top, I hold up my hands "Bailey, stop. No matter what you do, I do not want you back." Her eyes narrow, and her entire body language changes.

"Seriously? You would rather be with that lump than with me?" Her eyes light up when she insults Morgan, and it makes me want to throw the beer bottle against the wall. But I rein in the anger, taking a deep breath and closing my eyes.

"Morgan has nothing to do with this." I can't believe I'm even having this conversation. I should have listened to Matt when he told me to get rid of her months and months ago.

"She has everything to do with this! You broke up with me *because* of her!" she screams. I place my beer on the marble and fold my arms over my chest as I lean back against the kitchen counter. She's not wrong. I did. "So, you're not even going to deny it?" I take a deep breath, my hands going to my sides and grasping the edge of the counter behind me before I walk past her and out of the kitchen.

This is going to be a long day.

23

MORGAN

*T*he sun streams into my room through the crack in the curtains, and I smile, loving the sore feeling cascading through every limb of my body. Last night was something out of a dream, and no matter how many times Owen woke me up for rounds, two, three, and four, it still seems surreal. I look at the clock and notice that it's after eleven-thirty, I must have fallen asleep again after Owen left. As I sit up, the memory of him leaving feels almost like a dream, too.

Did I dream the whole thing? Was he even here last night? I wonder as I get up and head through the bedroom and into the living room, sinking down onto the couch. Out of the corner of my eye, I see my black dress abandoned on the hardwood floor, and it's then that I know it wasn't a dream. The way his fingers felt against the softness of my skin, the way my body molded to his as he took my mouth and devoured me whole.

The silence is deafening as I wait, wondering what I'm supposed to do now. Of all the things I was prepared for last night—the insecurities, the uncertainties, and the emotions—what I wasn't prepared for was waking up without him next to me. All I want is to lay next to him, feel him, and know that everything he said was true. I find my phone on the floor, and when I pick it up, I expect to see a text from Owen letting me know when he'll be done at the gym. Instead, there's nothing. The time display reminds me that it's been a few hours since he left, and as much as I try to shake the unsettling feeling coursing through me, I can't.

Before I think better of it, I pull up Owen's name and call, only for it to go straight to voicemail. The second I hear the beep, the sinking feeling sets in, and I take a deep breath, "Hey, Owen, umm, I just wanted to see when you'd be back." I hesitate a beat, then continue. "Call me when you get this."

Do not overreact, I think, hoping he's just with a client and everything's okay. I quickly pick up my cell once again and send a simple *call me* text to him, hoping he sees that in case he rarely listens to his phone messages.

Just as I head back into my bedroom, my phone vibrates, and I can't help the sense of hope that overtakes my body. I want it to be Owen. When I see that it's Allie, I try and cool the disappointment.

Allie: *Lunch, 20 minutes?*

I answer that I'll meet her at the store and go into my closet to find something to wear, not caring since I'll be back soon to change for my birthday party. Maybe lunch will be a distraction?

I can hope.

"WHAT'S WRONG?" Allie asks the second I step out of my car. I honestly thought I had a handle on my feelings, but the second I pulled up and saw that Owen's truck was nowhere to be seen, I realized that he might not actually be here like he said. "You okay?" Allie asks again as I try and curb the tears threatening to fall. I shake my head as I start walking to the front door, but at the last second, I turn and head toward the gym instead. "What are you doing?" Allie asks as she tries to keep up.

"I need to talk to Matt for a second," I say quickly

as I open the front door and head inside. Matt is manning the front desk, and the moment he sees me, his whole face breaks out into a huge smile.

"Well, if it isn't my favorite of Owen's girlfriends. What can I do for you, Morgan?"

"Have you seen Owen today?" My voice is quiet, and I don't know what I'm hoping for, but when he shakes his head, my heart sinks.

"No, I actually called him this morning, but he didn't answer, I wanted him to open the place for me." That heavy feeling starts to push against me as I look around the gym.

"So, he hasn't been by at all?" Matt shakes his head and the sense of dread hits its peak. He lied to me. Owen was never here.

Allie takes my hand, and when our eyes meet, hers beg for details. I shake my head, hoping she can wait a few more minutes.

"If you see him, can you let him know that I'm looking for him?" Matt eyes me with a weird look as I fight the tears again.

"Didn't he spend the night at your place?" he asks as Allie gasps next to me. I turn, hoping my look indicates that I don't want to talk about that right now. She gives me a subtle nod, and I breathe a sigh of relief that she understands. Matt eyes me once more, and his expression mirrors my confusion.

"Yeah, he stayed over. But he left early. Said he had to come to work…" From the puzzled look on Matt's face, I'd guess that's very unlike Owen.

"That's weird," he mutters, eyeing the floor as we stand in silence. "I'll be sure to tell him you're looking for him if I see him…" he says as I give him a grateful smile and head back out the door.

When I open the door to Hello Beautiful Boutique, I realize how grateful I am for Becca and her ability to just open the store without me being there to oversee her. Hiring her was the best decision I ever made.

"So, when were you going to tell me that Owen stayed over?" Allie says as the door shuts behind us, and the air-conditioning blasts me.

"I knew it!" Becca says from behind the front desk, winking in my direction as I roll my eyes and make my way to the back storage room. "I want details when you're not looking at me like you want to drown me in a kiddie pool." Although I appreciate her imagination, I wave her off, wanting nothing more than to distract myself from everything that is happening right now.

My entire body is taut with the conflicting

emotions warring inside my mind. On the one hand, the memories I have from last night create levity. Owen said he loved me. I'd spent most of my teens—and if I'm honest, most of the past few years—wanting nothing more than to know what those words felt like. But waking up to radio silence is almost like a dark cloud following me around on an otherwise sunny day.

I honestly don't know what to feel.

"Are you okay?" Allie asks, concern plastered all over her face. When our eyes meet, the tears form. "Oh, sweetie. Let's get out of here and talk, okay?" I nod my head because, at this point, I don't know what else to do.

"YOU'VE REACHED OWEN, *leave a message after the beep, or text me!*" His voice echoes in my ear as I look out my back window, staring at all the people gathered around the fire. I shut off my phone since there's no reason to leave yet another message. He hasn't responded to my last four or the half-dozen texts. After lunch with Allie, my sadness turned to anger—at Owen for ignoring me and not even giving me the time of day or courtesy of telling me what is more important than calling me. But mostly, I'm mad that I put myself in this position without even realizing it. After Aaron, I swore I'd never let a man cloud my judgment again. And here I am, breaking my own fucking rules.

"Still nothing?" Allie asks as Ben comes up behind her, placing his hands on her shoulders. The simplistic nature of the gesture should mean nothing, but over the last few weeks, I've become accustomed to Owen inadvertently touching my hand, my shoulder, grazing the side of my thigh. And because he's not here, and my heart is breaking into pieces across the tiled floor, those gestures are all I can see. Ben's eyes convey that Allie was not tight-lipped, but he just gives me a sad smile before kissing the side of her head and walking back outside to talk to Matt.

As I shake my head, I take my phone from my hand, putting it into my back pocket, hoping that the familiar feeling of deja vu doesn't worsen.

"Well, I brought you this to take your mind off it." She hands me a Jack and Coke, my favorite drink in college, one that I couldn't have for years because the smell brought me back to seedy bars, drunken nights, and mornings I wished I could forget.

"Just what I need…" I say, taking the drink from

her hand and downing it, placing the glass on the counter next to me.

"Whoa, okay," Allie mutters, taking my hand plus my empty glass as she leads me outside. "What you need to do is surround yourself with people who love you. Celebrate and then kick his ass when he decides to show up. Don't let him ruin this birthday. Not when I'm here." She gives me a wink, pouring enough Jack into my glass to warrant a warning. "Got it?" she asks, taking a shot glass and filling it to the brim. We toast, even though saying I'll enjoy the night and actually doing so are two very different things.

"To friendship," I say, a genuine smile crossing my face as Allie's eyes soften.

"To you." I smile at her response, not knowing what I would do without her.

It's been an hour, and I've tried my hardest to ignore my phone burning a hole in my back pocket. But every time there's a lull in conversation, it's all I can feel. Before I have a chance to think better of it, I excuse myself from the handful of friends still outside and head into the house. Once I close the door, I take out my cell and pull up the contact I've been trying to ignore all night.

Owen.

I hit call and pray I get an answer this time, even if it's not the one I want or accept. I just want some kind of resolution so I can feel like I'm back on solid ground. I'm so used to the ringing sound that I almost miss when the line connects, and a female voice answers.

"Can I help you?" the voice asks, and my brain tingles at the tone. For a split second, I wonder if I called the wrong number.

"Is Owen there?" I hate the way my voice cracks with uncertainty and the way my stomach drops when the woman sighs as if talking to me is a hardship to bear.

"No, he's not. He's busy, and probably will be for a while...if you know what I mean." She giggles, a sound that I know will resonate in the back of my mind for a long time, and then the line goes dead.

I don't remember falling to the floor, I don't remember Allie coming in and sitting in front of me, trying to get me to look at her. And I definitely don't remember Ben picking me up and walking me back to my bedroom where I stay until the sun comes up.

24

OWEN

It's been hours. We move from the kitchen, to the dining room then begrudgingly to the living room where I sit with my head in my hands, not knowing what else to do. The sun is starting to set, and I wonder if I'll ever get out of this house, knowing those photos aren't out in the world for others to see.

"Bailey, please. I'm begging you. All I want to do is protect her, so please let me delete the photos. That's all I want. As much as I want to deny that breaking up with you wasn't because of Morgan, I can't. Morgan and I have a history. We have a past. And I've been in love with her since I was sixteen." Bailey rolls her eyes, and I grab her shoulders, making her gaze meet mine. "I know it's hard to hear, but you need to get it through your head that we're done. Morgan was always the endgame; I just didn't know it." I also want to call my lawyer and get a restraining order for not only me but also Morgan, but that's for later. Right now, I just need to get those photos off her phone.

It didn't take me long to get it out of her how she got them. As it turns out, when she came into the gym the other day, she snatched my phone off the front desk while I was hiding in the back. She said she wasn't looking for anything in particular, but when she found the photos, she sent them to herself and put my phone back where I left it.

It's almost as if I have no idea who this woman is. This is not the woman I asked out last year, and it's definitely not the woman I thought I loved only a few months ago. "Bails…" I hope using her nickname gets through to her more than the yelling has so far. "I know I hurt you, and that's on me. But, blackmail? That's not how this goes, that's not how this ends."

As she sits on the lounge chair opposite me, her knees pinned to her chest, I wonder if I actually got through to her at all.

"So, how does this end then? You happily in love, and me rotting on the sidelines? I don't think so." Apparently, a rational response was too much to ask.

"I'm not asking for much here, Bailey. All I'm asking for is for you to delete those photos. I've stayed here for hours because I want to do this the easy way." Her eyebrow quirks in question, and I just shake my head and continue. "The easy way is me asking you to delete the photos and you doing the right thing." She scoffs as if that's the furthest thing from her mind. "The hard way is me getting my lawyer involved and taking you to court. Filing a harassment charge, as well as defamation of character and blackmail." I think the gravity of the situation finally sinks in, yet from the defiant look in her eyes, it's clear she knows that it's her only leverage, and if she gives it up, it's done.

"You wouldn't do that," she croaks, getting up from the chair and pacing the room. I stand, making her stop in her tracks as she watches me make my way toward her. She backs up, hitting the wall behind her as I cage her in.

"Try me," I mutter through clenched teeth.

"If you were serious, you wouldn't have spent the last few hours with me instead of with *her*." She's right. I tried to avoid the legal route because it could get messy, fast. But right now, I'm praying for a miracle.

"I gotta piss," I say, walking away and heading to

the bathroom to catch my breath and figure out what to do next. I'm trying not to think of Morgan and what she's probably thinking right now. I know she's likely wondering where I am. I know she's probably sent me a million texts and messages, asking me to call her back. And the overwhelming sense of guilt that crashes over me at the thought of her thinking that I don't love her, imagining that I don't want every part of her forever, sends me into a tailspin.

Fuck it, I think, staring at my reflection in the mirror. *I'm done being the nice guy.* I make my way back into the kitchen and hear Bailey on the phone.

"Can I help you?" She pants, voice sultry, and from where I'm standing, she looks smug. I wonder who she's talking to. "No, he's not. He's busy, and probably will be for a while...if you know what I mean." Her giggle sends nausea coursing through my entire being, and it hits me like a Mack truck who she's talking to—and the fact that she's on my phone.

"What the fuck are you doing?" My voice rises as I make my way toward her, and as she drops my phone onto the counter. I see Morgan's name on the display, and I silently curse my stupidity. Bailey shrugs her shoulders as if what she did wasn't that bad, and that's when the tether breaks. This is the moment I stop caring about creating problems for her. This is the moment I stop caring about Bailey altogether. "Get the fuck out of my house. Now." I point to the front door, but she doesn't move. I lean over and look her directly in the eye. "Did I stutter?" I press as she gives me a cocky smirk.

"Nope. But I want to remind you that those photos are still right here." She takes her phone from her back pocket and shakes it in my face. "And if I leave, then they get sent to *everyone*." God give me the strength to not throw this woman out my door with my bare hands.

"If you do not get out of my house right now, I will call the cops and have you arrested for trespassing."

"You wouldn't dare," she murmurs, and I just stand there with my hands on my hips, waiting.

"Try me."

She huffs as she collects her things and begrudgingly walks to the front of the house. She turns as she opens the door and says, "You will regret this, Owen." I shake my head as I place my hand on her back and push her out the door.

"You'll be hearing from my lawyer in the morning." I slam the door in her face and take the first real breath I have since I woke up this morning to find her text.

* * *

I'M STANDING on Morgan's front porch, hoping to God she answers because I've tried to call her a million times, and every time, it goes straight to voicemail.

Karma's a bitch, I guess.

"Come on, Morgan, open the door," I mutter as I continue to knock and ring the doorbell.

"She's not here," a guy says from behind me as I turn and see a man that looks familiar, but I can't place him. I know I've heard that British accent before, though.

"What do you mean, she's not here? Where is she?" I ask, a sense of panic settling into the pit of my stomach.

The man shakes his head and steps forward, handing me a Polaroid.

"That's not for me to say," he says, walking back to his car. When he drives away, my eyes move down to take in the photo he just handed me. When I see the picture of Allie with Morgan, a cake in front of them, that's the moment my whole world comes crashing down.

Tonight was Morgan's birthday party.

I missed it.

Just like Aaron.

25

MORGAN

I'm sitting in my room, and Allie and Ben are still downstairs, waiting. I don't know what they're waiting for exactly...me to feel better? Me to let them know that it's okay to come in since I'm not bursting into tears anymore? None of that is bound to happen in the next few minutes, so I pull out my phone and text Kennedy, a little wary of calling my therapist at night, but knowing that she told me it was okay.

Me: *Can I call you? Really need to talk.*

What else do I say without spilling the whole story? And, honestly, I'm in no mood to type that out.

Instead of answering my text, my phone vibrates, and her picture shows up, letting me know she's calling. When I answer, I spill everything. What happened with Owen last night, waking up alone and him ghosting me the entire day. I end on the bit about hearing the girl on his phone. That's when she takes a deep breath.

"Morgan, those panicked feelings are natural. Any woman who hears another woman's voice on her boyfriend's phone is going to freak out." I go to say something, but she continues. "But from what we've talked about regarding Owen and your relationship, I need to ask if you actually think he would cheat on you."

"I don't know. I didn't think so," I say honestly, feeling the tears forming once again. I lean my head back against the headboard, wondering how this went to complete shit so fast.

"Nope, that's not an answer. You know in your heart what the answer is." I exhale, hating that she's right.

"Even if I know he wouldn't cheat, why do I still feel like my h-heart was r-ripped right out of my c-chest?" I stutter with my sobs. My heart rate rises, my hands start to shake, and my breathing becomes shallow.

"Morgan, I need you to breathe for me, okay? In through the mouth, out through the nose, remember?" I nod my head, not even thinking about the fact that she can't see me as I take gulping breaths, trying to get my panic attack to cease. When it tempers, Kennedy is still on the line.

"All of the feelings you have inside of you are valid. Every single one is true and needs to be addressed. But you need to clear your head first. You need to get away from the thoughts that are screaming at you."

"How do I do that?" I whisper, finally feeling my breaths come more evenly as I close my eyes.

"Get away for a few days. Try and be with people who care about you but have no association with Owen. And, most importantly, talk. Talk to someone besides me. Someone that knows you and cares about you no matter what. Remember, those are the people that will lift you up in times of crisis."

"Do you think I'm overreacting?" I've had that thought ever since I hung up the phone on who I assume was Bailey, even though I don't know for sure. "What if this is just me projecting what happened last year onto Owen?"

"It's a valid point, and one I think you should think about. But I want to reiterate that you *do* need to talk to Owen, as well. Just talking to your friends and family won't fix this. Me telling you to clear your head is a way for you to talk to Owen with an open mind, ready to hear what he has to say. And from what you're telling me right now, you're not there yet. So, take some time, evaluate everything that happened, and then hear him out."

She's right.

And I know just the place to do that.

"THANKS FOR LETTING me stay here for a few days," I mumble into the teacup that Allie just placed in my hand. Convincing her to let me accompany her back to New Orleans wasn't hard. Convincing her to do it last night when my emotions were at their peak? That was another story. She thought I was overreacting. I told her I needed breathing room from Owen and everything that reminded me of him.

"You can come and visit anytime. But you know this won't solve anything." She takes a sip from her own mug, smirking over the rim. I nod my head because it's true. I'm only delaying the inevitable.

"I just needed some time away," I say, leaning back and looking around, remembering the surprise on my face when we pulled up to her house and I saw that it was yellow. That was something I didn't expect. *I think it's cute*, Allie said. I agree, it *is* cute, along with her décor, which displays her personality to a T. "Do you spend any time here at all?" I ask, knowing that she bounces between New Orleans and London. "I know your love will always be your store." She nods, taking a sip of her tea and grimacing for the fourth time.

"God, I miss coffee." A laugh bubbles out of me as I sit up and she places the still full mug on the table beside her.

"If you hate it so much, why do you drink it?" I ask, loving the small blush that forms on her cheeks.

"I will always love coffee over everything, that's a given. But Ben loves his *cuppa,* and when we're in London, it's a common thing to have tea several times a day, so I'm trying to like it."

"And I'm guessing it's not going well?" She shakes her head as I breathe in the scent of the Earl Grey that's warming my hands.

"I've tried almost every kind on the planet, and I still can't stand to take more than a few sips." She starts laughing as I set my cup down. She takes my hand in hers. "Are you okay?"

How do I answer that? Right now, I feel all right, but it hits me in waves. I could be sitting just like this and then, all of sudden, I'll remember what happened yesterday and how Bailey's voice sounded on the phone, and everything comes crashing back to reality.

"I don't know," I say honestly. "It was like deja vu all over again, and yet it hurt more this time."

"Of course, it did," Allie says, crossing her legs and twisting her body to face mine on the couch. "You love Owen more than you loved Aaron." I avert my eyes because admitting that I actually loved Owen after what happened almost seems wrong.

"He told me he loved me last night," I admit for the first time out loud. Allie's eyes bulge, and her mouth opens in surprise.

"Okay, that changes everything!" I look at her dumbfounded because it doesn't make a lick of difference. Actually, it kind of makes it worse. "Morgan, he wouldn't have told you he loved you if he was sleeping around." The thought had crossed my mind, but last night I was so caught up in old feelings and desperations that I just needed to leave. Now, I'm wondering if I should have stayed and talked to him.

"You think I should have stayed." She tilts her head to the side, and I roll my eyes. "So, you think that he did nothing wrong?" My defenses are going up, and Allie can sense it, so she moves a bit closer and places her hands on my knees.

"I think you should have talked to him. I know what he did was wrong, and honestly, someone like Owen would never do something like that unless there was a reason." I take a deep breath as she continues. "You have every right to be upset and hurt right now, but don't throw everything away because of this. Talk it out. See what he says and then take it from there."

If only it were that easy.

"I THOUGHT we were going to Hello Beautiful Boutique?" I ask, walking down a road that is so packed, I wonder if it's a state holiday I didn't know about or something. I have been asking all morning to go and see Allie's store. I haven't had the chance to see it yet, and honestly, I'm kind of nervous to see what she loves compared to what I do. I know she tells me all the time that she loves the Miami store, and I do too, it's my baby. But seeing her vision is something completely different.

"We are. I just want to get something to eat first." Allie winks as we continue walking. I love the atmosphere and basking in the sun. I pray that the humidity stays away, but I know that is a futile wish.

"Eat? We just had breakfast?" This girl makes no sense sometimes. She gives me a look and takes my hand, walking faster toward a place called Cafe Du Monde. The green and white awning catches my eye, and so does the line that seems to go on forever. "We're seriously going to stand in that line?" I mutter. I'm not really in the mood, even if the food is *orgasmic* as she put it.

"Trust me. It's worth it." My side-eye is strong as we stand at the back of the line. I can feel the rising heat beating down on the back of my neck. "Have you ever had beignets before?" I shake my head and wonder if that's what all these people are here for. Allie smirks and links her arm with mine. "You are going to wish I never took you here. Because from today on, you will only want these for all meals." I roll my eyes, not really understanding why she's so hung up on doughnuts, but I'll give it a shot.

We finally get our baskets of fried dough covered in powdered sugar and for a split second, my eyes scan the crowd for someone watching me eat. I shake that feeling away, knowing that no one gives a shit what I put in my mouth. Speaking of, the moment that pastry hits my tongue, I know I will never be the same, and everything Allie said was true.

"Ermagaw," I exclaim around a mouthful of Heaven. "How do you not live here?" She laughs, taking another huge bite and wiping off the excess sugar from around her mouth.

"Trust me, I actively stop myself from coming here daily." I burst out laughing as we start walking, and I feel my phone vibrate in my back pocket. When I take it out and see it's Owen, I hit ignore and put the phone back where it belongs.

"Still ignoring him?" Allie asks, avoiding my eyes as I sigh loudly, throwing away my empty basket and wiping my hands, not wanting to get powdered sugar on my clothes.

"I'm not ready to talk to him yet." I can see her trying to say something, but I stop her before she can get it out. "Before you say that I need to buck up and do it, I know. I just need to get my bearings first. So, spare me the lecture, okay?" She holds up her hands in mock surrender, and we continue on our way to Hello Beautiful Boutique in silence.

A vibration letting me know that a voicemail has come through burns a hole in my back pocket, and I fight hard to keep my hands from grabbing it and listening to what he has to say.

26

MORGAN

"*M, baby I'm so sorry. I never meant to leave you like that, I never meant to miss your birthday. I fucked up. I know that, but please let me explain. You don't ever have to forgive me, just please let me hear your voice. Please let me know you're okay.*" There's a second of silence before he whispers, "*I love you. Remember that. I love you so fucking much.*" And then the line goes dead. I save the message for the fifth time and hit the icon that lets me listen to it again.

I know this isn't healthy. But right now, hearing his voice both soothes and burns me at the same time. Once the message is over again, I look at his texts, all of them begging me to answer him. As my fingers hover over the keys, I wonder what I'd say.

He wants to know if I'm okay, and right now, I don't know the answer to that. I don't know where to go from here. Eventually, I have to get back to reality, and unfortunately, that means running Hello Beautiful Boutique, which happens to be located right next to his gym. The irony isn't lost on me.

"What are you still doing up?" Ben says, coming down the stairs and heading into the kitchen. I watch as he takes a glass out of the cupboard and fills it with water then leans back against the counter as his eyes watch me over the rim of the glass. I shrug my shoulders and grip my phone in my hands like it's my lifeline. "You still haven't talked to him?" My eyes question him because I know Allie told him everything, I just never expected him to confront me about it.

"What would I say?" I admit, needing some kind of guidance at this point because hiding out a few states away won't make sense forever.

"Does it matter? I bet he just wants to hear your voice." Ben comes into the living room and sits on the couch next to me. "Coming from someone who knows what it's like to lose something they love, that's all he wants right now." I nod, knowing he's talking about when he and Allie were separated, but this is different. "What are you so scared of?" he asks bluntly, and it catches me off guard. As much as I've analyzed the situation, that question has never come up.

"I don't know," I admit, but he shakes his head.

"Nope. You know the answer. What are you scared of?" God, no wonder he does this for a living. He's good.

"I guess I'm scared of knowing the truth." He nods, motioning for me to continue. "When Aaron left, I knew what he did. And if I'm honest with myself, I never loved him the way a fiancée should. But this time is different..."

"Because you love Owen more than you loved Aaron?" I nod, smiling because Allie said the exact same thing. "You know love isn't something to be scared of. Sure, it can be scary sometimes, but it can also be fulfilling and a feeling unlike anything else on this Earth."

"Being loved by Owen isn't the scary part. I've dreamt about that since I was sixteen. It's..."

"It's the fact that he broke your heart when you thought he was the one person you didn't think would." I nod because he gets it. That's exactly what's coursing through me right now. I know deep down that Owen didn't sleep with Bailey, but he *did* ignore me and shut me out, and that's something I'm having a hard time getting over. Before I can stop them, the tears start to form and fall freely down my cheeks. Just as Ben gets up to make his way over to me, Allie comes into the room and wraps her arms around me.

"You should talk to him," Ben says, touching his hand to my shoulder. "Even if it ends, at least you'll know." I take a shaky breath before I nod, watching as Ben gives Allie a light kiss before heading back upstairs, leaving us alone.

"You want a drink?" Allie whispers in my ear, and I laugh as I shake my head. As much as I would love to drown my sorrows in a bottle of wine, I know I need to face this. "How about some retail therapy? I happen to know a good place to shop." She gives me a wink, and I look into her eyes and thank God that I have someone in my life who cares about me enough to stay up past midnight and hold me while I cry, then take me shopping because she knows I need a distraction. It doesn't hurt that she looks at me like I'm the only important thing in her life—at least in this moment.

"I think it's a bit late for retail therapy," I tease, looking at the clock on the stove to see that it's after one in the morning.

"Well, I do own the place. So, technically if you

wanted to, we *could* go shopping…" We both laugh, knowing that the idea is absurd.

"I think I can wait until tomorrow." She nods and holds my face between her palms, wiping away the stray tears.

"You okay for now?" I smile, loving that she added the *for now* because it's true. Right now, I'm okay. But in five minutes, that could change. I love her for acknowledging it.

"Right now, I'm good. Thanks." She smiles, wrapping me in her arms and hugging me way too tightly.

"I love you forever. No matter what happens." I hug her tighter as the warm feeling of her embrace cascades over my entire body until I feel my eyes grow heavy. I know I need to head to bed.

Tomorrow is a new day. The day I face the reality I've been hiding from, the one that could break me in two if I let it. But I refuse to let that happen. No matter what.

27

OWEN

She's been gone for two days. The amount of times I've bothered not only Morgan's parents but also Becca at the store is becoming a problem. I know I fucked up. I know I need to grovel for the rest of my life because the idea of losing her when I just finally found her again is tearing me to pieces.

I've been lying in this bed, wondering what my next move will be for hours, when my phone goes off on the bedside table. When I pick it up, I see that it's after one in the morning and I question who the fuck would be calling me at this hour. The phone number isn't one I recognize, so when I pick it up, I'm surprised to discover who it is.

"You need to come get your girl." The British

accent rings through my ears, and I wrack my brain trying to figure out who it is.

"Excuse me?" I ask, the weight of the last few days falling over me once again.

"Owen, it's been two days. As much as I understand her needing space, I need you to come and get her. You need to make a move here, because she won't. And I can't say I blame her after what you did." It finally clicks who the voice belongs to: Allie's husband. This must be who handed me that Polaroid outside her house the night of the party.

"Where is she?" I ask, having a feeling I know but needing confirmation.

"New Orleans." I close my eyes, feeling relief wash over me. I know where she is. I can find her. "She's staying at our house. And as much as I love that girl, I miss my alone time with my wife."

"I've been trying to find her since that night. No one will tell me anything," I admit, getting up from bed and heading over to where my laptop is plugged into the wall. I open it, pulling up a browser to look for flights to New Orleans.

"Do you blame them?" I sigh, knowing I have a lot of groveling ahead of me.

"I know you won't believe me, but I was trying to protect her. My ex was trying to blackmail me, and by extension, Morgan. I didn't want any of it to touch her, so I tried to deal with it myself."

"And how did that work out for you?" When I don't respond, he sighs. "Owen, I know you love her. I know you did what you did to protect her, even though you went about it all wrong." I roll my eyes and scroll through flight after flight, trying to find the earliest one possible. "But that girl loves you. And if you get here and talk to her, I guarantee that you will be able to work things out."

"How are you so sure?" I ask, not knowing why he has confidence in me or Morgan's ability to forgive me.

"Because when I talk to Morgan, I can see she's hurting. But behind the anger and sadness is still love. She's torn between wanting to hate you and knowing she loves you. She just needs an explanation for what you did." God, I hope I get the chance to give her one.

"I found a flight. I'll be there by tonight," I mutter, feeling my heart start to race, and my hands begin to clam up.

"Good." He rattles off his address so I know where to go before he says, "I hope she forgives you. But remember, she has every right not to." He hangs up before I have a chance to respond. And honestly, what could I have said? He's right, I just need to find a way to explain everything without fucking everything up—again.

* * *

I GET to the gym and open the door to find Matt leaning back in the chair behind the desk, throwing a tennis ball into the air.

"Am I interrupting?" I ask, chuckling as he almost falls over at the sound of my voice.

"Way to scare a guy to death," he mutters, throwing the ball in my direction. I catch it easily and throw it back. "What are you doing here? I thought you'd still be bothering Morgan's parents, trying to figure out where she is."

"I know where she is. That's why I'm here." He gets up and walks around the side of the desk, stopping directly in front of me.

"Well? Where is she?" No matter what he says, he's been worried these last few days, too. He knows how much Morgan means to me, and when everything went down, and he saw how badly I reacted to the whole thing, he became invested.

"New Orleans." His eyes widen as he leans against the desk.

"Why the hell is she there? That's like three states away!"

"Yes, thank you, Captain Obvious."

"Why did she go there?" I remind him Allie lives there and understanding begins to sink in. "Okay, so you're going after her, right?" he says, absentmindedly playing with the ball in his hands.

"Of course. I just wanted to come in and make sure you were okay with it." He gives me a look, telling me it's a stupid question, but I shake it off. "Plus, I needed to go over my schedule for the next couple of days and cancel a few appointments." Matt shakes his head.

"Don't cancel anything. I'll take your clients for the next few days."

"No way. You've been booked solid since we opened. You can't take on my shit, too." He waves me off and goes back around the desk, turning on the computer. After a few minutes of silence, he types a few things and then sits back in the chair with his hands behind his head.

"Done. You now have no appointments until next week." I must not hide my surprise well because he laughs, leaning forward on the desk. "Dude, I love doing this. I know the clients that can change days and times, so I emailed them and asked if they could.

Now, no matter what they say, I will make it work. Go get your girl and bring her back here, because I think Becca next door needs a break—or a night out." I laugh, shaking my head. "Plus, you are not very fun when you're like this. So, please, get her and come home happy, okay?"

"I'll do my best."

I PULL into the driveway of a cute yellow house that looks like it's something out of a catalogue. From what little I know about Allie, it suits her. As I step out of my car, the front door opens, and when Ben steps out, my heart drops. I was hoping it would be Morgan, but I know that would have been the best-case scenario. This is reality.

"Where's Morgan?" I ask, walking up the front steps and onto the porch. Ben puts out his hand, and I grasp it.

"Out for lunch with Allie. They should be back soon. You got here quick," he says, looking at his watch. I took the first flight I found that got me here as quickly as possible. I didn't even have time to find a hotel. I just rented a car, punched in this address, and drove, knowing that the faster I got here, the sooner I could see Morgan.

"Yeah, I didn't really want to chance getting here tomorrow, so I booked the first flight I saw." He nods, just as a car pulls into the driveway. "That them?" I ask, not turning around. I don't want to risk Morgan running, or worse, asking Allie to drive away.

"Yeah, you can turn around. She knows it's you." His head nods toward the car, and as I turn around and my eyes catch Morgan's, everything around me stops. *Fuck, she looks so beautiful.* In her rolled-up blue jeans, flowy white tank top, and her hair in that messy bun that drives me crazy, she looks stunning.

Before I have a chance to say a word, she raises her hand, stopping me from talking. Ben chuckles behind me and whispers, "Good luck, man," as he and Allie head inside.

"What are you doing here?" Morgan asks, standing a good six feet from me as I desperately try to control my need to take steps toward her.

"Ben called—" I start as her eyes dart to the front window where I know both Ben and Allie are watching. "He just wanted me to know that you were okay, and he told me to come and get you." Her eyes narrow as if what I just said offends her somehow.

"He told you to come get me?" The hurt in her voice is palpable, and I realize what I just insinuated and start to shake my head.

"No, baby, no. He doesn't want to get rid of you. He just wants us to work things out. And he knew that I needed to explain myself, so he told me where you were." Her gaze is glued to the ground, her hands in her pockets as she shifts from foot to foot. "I was so worried..." Morgan cackles, rolling her eyes at the same time.

"Yeah, right. You didn't really miss me when you ignored me and didn't answer any of my calls or texts. It was hours, Owen. Not just one but *several*." I take a step toward her, ready to explain everything, but she holds up her hand again. "You know what? I don't think I'm ready to hear your excuses right now. Just go." I stand there numbly, dumbfounded that the woman I love dismissed me without a second thought.

Not happening.

"No, I'm not leaving." She tries to walk around me, but my fingers grip her arm, holding her in place. "Morgan, I love you. More than anything on this Earth. More than my gym. More than my life."

She starts to shake under my touch, so I let her go, hoping to God she doesn't walk away. When she doesn't, I continue. "I fucked up. But not in the way you think. All I'm asking for is a chance to explain."

"Fine. You have ten minutes." She sits on the front step, her eyes staring me down as I sit next to her. When she moves an inch to the right, my stomach sinks.

I have a lot of work to do.

MORGAN

*W*hy does he have to look so edible? It's not fair that he shows up and it looks like it's laundry day, and I'm wearing the most unflattering thing imaginable. But here he is, in his basketball shorts, t-shirt, and backwards ball cap that he knows drives me crazy, looking like he wants to devour me whole. How am I supposed to resist him when he looks at me with those blue eyes that turn me to mush, no matter how hard I try?

"I didn't cheat on you." His voice is soft, and I almost don't hear it, but when I look over, his eyes plead with mine to understand.

"I know," I admit. Being here with Allie, away from everything and everyone that reminds me of what happened, I realized that Bailey answering his phone was a ploy. A reason for me to doubt him when I know in my gut that he would never do that.

"If you know, then why did you come here?" It's a valid question, one I asked myself a million times, and one that Allie asked to the point of me wanting to strangle her.

"I guess I just needed space. Time away from you and the shop to gather my thoughts. Plus, I really didn't want to run into Bailey and have her make everything worse." He nods, still not saying much. "What happened, Owen? You left me to wake up alone, you told me you would be there that night. You told me you were nothing like Aaron, and yet you did the exact same thing he did." He starts shaking his head.

"I am nothing like him. I didn't cheat on you like he did." I nod, because that's true. But when I turn on the step and face him, I know he sees the seriousness, and his expression falls.

"Regardless, you betrayed me just like he did. You might not have cheated on me, but you still lied to me, ignored me, and left me alone to think the worst. And coming from you? The man I've loved since I was sixteen? That was almost worse." He lets his head fall into his hands as his fingers dig into his scalp. My hands itch to touch him, but I know the moment I do, I'll cave. And I need to hear what he has to say.

"She was blackmailing me." My eyes look over at him, confused. "She somehow got ahold of my phone and found the pictures you sent." My eyes furrow, not understanding what he's saying. Then his eyes meet mine, and it dawns on me—the lingerie photos. My gut wrenches. "That's exactly why I didn't tell you. Because I wanted to keep that look of horror off your face. I didn't want this to touch you."

"That's not up to you, Owen. If you want to do this with me, then you need to be *with* me, not always in front of me. We're a team, and that means I need to know when something like this affects not only you but also me." He nods, his eyes meeting mine once more.

"I felt sick when she texted me that morning. I hated leaving you after what we shared. That was the best night of my life, and she ruined it."

"She didn't ruin anything. If you had just talked to me, I would have told you to tell her to go fuck herself."

"What?" His shocked expression releases a chuckle, and a small smile crosses my lips.

"Does her having those photos make me angry?

Hell fucking yes, it does. Is it an invasion of privacy? Of course. But is it the end of the world? No." He eyes me, seemingly confused.

"But she was going to send those pictures to everyone she knew..." I take my hand and place it over his, feeling a tremor go through him as I do.

"Owen, honey, who could she have possibly sent them to that would ruin my life, hmm?" His brow furrows as he thinks it over, and I place my hand on the side of his face, a feeling of relief washing over me because I know that everything will be okay. "The papers? Bloggers? Social media? All of that means nothing to me."

"But what about the store?" I tilt my head to the side, thinking about what something like that could do to the reputation of Hello Beautiful Boutique. I look over my shoulder and see Allie peering out through the window. When she winks at me, I smile, knowing that if anything happened, she'd be right there with me, helping.

"I'm not the store. I just run it. Those pictures represent something important for me." Owen gets closer, his knees touching mine, and it takes all my restraint not to kiss him right here, right now. "When I put on that white lace..." He groans, his fingers digging into my leg as if he's reliving it.

"When I put that on, I felt the sexiest I have ever felt in my entire life."

"Baby, you are the sexiest woman on this planet." His hand grasps the side of my neck, and he pulls me forward so our foreheads touch. The warm caress of his breath washes over my lips, making it even harder to resist him.

"You hurt me," I whisper, those uncertainties rising once again with him this close. I want to forgive him. With every fiber of my being, I want to wrap myself in his arms and tell him that I'll forget all of it. But that's not reality. The truth is, he betrayed me. Maybe not intentionally, but he still did it.

"I know. And I have to live with that for the rest of my life." His eyes are dark as his lips get closer and closer. "I swore when you told me what that bastard did to you in New York that I would never betray you like that. And I did. I will spend the rest of my life making up for the fact that I made you doubt my love for you. I made you doubt that you are the single best thing in my life. And that guts me, cuts me to the core. I'm so sorry, baby. So fucking sorry." I can't help the tears that fall as he says those words, and before I can say anything back, his lips are on mine, and the whole world falls away.

Yes, we have a lot to work through. Yes, we still need to talk about exactly what happened and how we're going to get those pictures away from his ex. But right now, I need this feeling. I need to remember what his lips feel like against mine, I need to remember what his hands feel like grasping my hair and pulling me closer as he devours me. When his tongue demands entrance, I know I'm a goner, and the groan that escapes from deep in his throat makes me realize that he feels it, too. Before I can say anything, Owen lifts me off the stairs and places me on his lap, his arms encircling my waist as I start to grind against him, losing myself to the feeling of being back in his arms.

"Ahem!" someone says from behind Owen, and when we part, breaths heaving, and I look, I start laughing. Allie stands there with her arms crossed, Ben right behind her, a huge smile on both their faces. "As much as I love that you've made up, please refrain from giving my neighbors a show they normally have to pay a monthly subscription for." The blush travels up my cheeks as I bury my head against Owen's shoulder.

"Sorry," Owen grumbles and stands with me still in his arms. "I'll take her somewhere else then." He kisses the side of my head as I wave goodbye to Allie, who motions for me to call her. I smile, nodding as Owen puts me in his rental car, kissing me one last time before closing the door.

"Where are we going?" I ask as he gets in, starts the car, and then backs out of the driveway.

"Well, since I didn't have time to find a place to sleep, I say we start there. Then once I have you alone, I'm gonna show you exactly what you mean to me." A shiver runs down my spine as his hand covers mine, holding tight.

As much as we need to talk, the sexual tension in the car is palpable, and I know the minute he has me alone, there won't be much talking.

29

OWEN

The second I shut the door to the hotel room, Morgan is in my arms. I push her against the wall, feeling her mold to me as my lips find hers.

"Fuck, baby, I missed you…" I ground out as my lips travel down her neck and past the scoop neck of her shirt as I start to devour her right then and there. Her fingers find their way into my hair, and my hands grip her hips, pulling her close so she feels just how turned on I am to have her back in my arms.

"Owen," she moans, and the second my name leaves her lips, everything around me slows. I didn't think I would ever hear her say my name like that again. Hearing her say it while pulling me closer, clearly wanting my lips on every part of her skin, makes me thank the universe for allowing me this second chance. "Please..." she begs as my fingers find the hem of her tank top, lightly brushing against her skin as her head falls back against the wall with a thud. Gone is the insecurity I saw that first night. Gone are the thoughts of her so-called imperfections that only she seems to see. All that's left is a woman who drives me crazy just by breathing, and I plan to spend the rest of my life reminding her of that fact— no matter what gets in our way.

I'm thrust back to reality when Morgan's fingers find the side of my face as she brings my gaze back to hers, brushing her lips softly against mine. She slows the pace to one of molasses, leaving me groaning against her lips, wanting more. So much more.

"M, baby, you're driving me crazy," I mutter as she smiles against my lips. And before I have a chance to beg even more, her hands rest on my chest, pushing me away. Just as I open my mouth to complain, she shakes her head, her fingers playing with the edge of her top. Before I have a chance to beg her to take it off, it's flying to the floor, leaving me with the sight of utter perfection. She's wearing a white lace bra that reminds me way too much of the outfit that started all of this, and I groan, my mouth watering. Her nipples pucker under my gaze, and my hands itch to touch her.

"You can't be real," I whisper, and from her intake of breath, I realize I said that out loud. I give her one of my best smiles as my fingers trace patterns across her stomach and up to the bottom of her bra. "Seriously, you have no idea what you look like right now. It's like I sold my soul to the devil. And I would do it again if I got to look at you forever." Her shy smile lets me know that I need to say shit like that to her more often, because my goal is for her to know that every fucking day for the rest of her life.

"Kiss me," she demands, her hands gripping the sides of my face. I'm not one to deny my woman what she wants, so I go willingly. When her lips find mine, my hands find the clasp of her bra. When it's discarded on the floor along with her top, I start kissing down the column of her neck, past her collarbone, and stop just above her nipples. I glance up, catching her eyes as her breathing increases. I give her a smirk just before my lips surround one of her turgid peaks, making her hips buck against mine, eliciting a sound I've never heard from her throat.

"Owen...*shit*," she mutters as her fingers find purchase in the strands of my hair, pulling me closer as I give the other breast the same attention. Her hips grind against me, trying to find something to relieve the tension I'm sure, but when she groans in frustration, I can't help but let out a laugh that has her pulling my head back so our eyes meet.

"Owen, don't make me beg," she says through gritted teeth. And who am I to deny her? So, I do the one thing I've been dreaming about since I left that morning. I sink to my knees, loving the flare of desire that crosses her face as my fingers find the waistband of her jeans. I unbutton and unzip and let them fall to the floor. I groan the minute I see the matching white lace panties that cover the pussy I've been thinking about since the moment I first had a taste.

"You gonna let me taste you, baby?" I ask, not really waiting for an answer before I gently slide them off her hips, watching them fall to the floor with the rest of her clothes as the scent of her arousal hits me. "Fuck, look at you," I mutter, not wasting any time before my mouth moves up her thighs with open-mouthed kisses. When she steps out of her jeans and panties, I take one of her legs and place it over my shoulder then go in for the kill.

"Shit!" she screams as my lips surround her heat,

my tongue teasing her clit as Morgan's hips buck against my face.

"Fuck, baby, ride my face," I say, and she does just that. Her hips grind against me as my tongue plunges as far as it can go into her heat, making her knees buckle, and her fingers grip my hair even harder.

This…right here.

This is all I need from her. Having her at my mercy, her on the cusp of orgasm as my lips taste her sweet arousal. *Fucking Heaven.*

I know the second she goes over the edge because her entire body locks, her fingers digging into my scalp to the point of pain. But I don't let up. I take her there, my tongue flicking her clit relentlessly as her body starts to shake, the orgasm taking over every part of her beautiful face. She screams my name just as I plunge two fingers into her heat, causing another, even bigger orgasm to overtake her. I groan against her, trying to think of anything but the sounds she emits, because I don't want to come in my pants like a teenager—not again, at least.

After she finally comes down from her state of bliss, I wipe my mouth against her skin and kiss up her body, loving how relaxed she is against me. I expected her to be sated, blissful, and relaxed, but I see determination in her eyes.

"Now it's my turn," she says, kissing me hard, sending arousal straight to my dick that gets even harder, leaving me lightheaded. My eyes track her as she lowers to her knees, an image that will forever be ingrained in my memories because this right here, Morgan in front of me, unbuttoning my jeans as I shuck my shirt to the floor, taking my cock in her small hands and looking up as if to ask permission is something I didn't know I could have. And now I know exactly what Heaven looks like.

It looks just like her.

"Fuck, baby, you don't have to do this," I say, knowing full well I won't be able to stop her but wanting her to know that this isn't what I wanted or expected. But from the sly smile on her face, she's not stopping. With rapt attention, her lips part, and the second her warmth surrounds my cock, my hands fly out in front of me, landing on the wall, holding me upright. Because this feeling right here? It's pure bliss.

"Morgan, baby. *Shit,* yes just like that…" I moan. Loving the way her lips feel around me, adoring how her fingers play with my shaft as I barrel closer and closer to the release that's coming way too soon.

"You keep doing that, and I'm gonna come in your mouth." The moment I say it, I know that's not what I want. As much as I love the feel of her mouth around me, I want to feel her pussy surrounding me even more. So, with every ounce of restraint I have, I pull myself away from her. From the pout on her sweet lips, I know she doesn't like my decision.

"I wasn't done!" I give her a smirk as I place my hands under her arms and pull her up, taking her lips in a punishing kiss.

"I am not fucking coming in your mouth. Not today. Today, I need to feel you surrounding me as I fuck you. I need that, baby." She nods, her lips taking mine as I spin us around, stepping out of my pants and pushing her back onto the bed. She retreats to the center, propping up on her elbows, and at that moment, I know she is the best decision I ever made.

30

MORGAN

*T*he way he's looking at me in this moment makes me feel like the only person in the world. His eyes take in every part of me as I lay on the bed, waiting. He's a dream, standing there with his erect cock standing at attention like a beacon to my pleasure. I never knew sex could be like this, so intimate, so passionate that you lose all track of time. And I know it's Owen. It's how he looks at me, the way he holds me close when no one else is watching. And his love for me.

"Fuck, Morgan, you can't look at me like that. I'll come before we even start." I smirk, knowing I can't help the way I'm looking at him. He's everything I knew he would be and more, and the more time I spend with him, the more I want.

"Are you just going to stand there and stare?" I ask, loving the heat that flashes in his eyes.

"Oh, baby, I could stand here all day and just look at you. Just thinking about you gets me off. But right now, I need to be inside you." I nod because that sounds like an amazing plan. Before I have a chance to complain that he's taking too long, he crawls onto the bed, over me, and settles between my legs. His cock is at my entrance, and the more I move, the more it hits my clit every time, sending my eyes rolling to the back of my head.

"Fuck..." I groan as the heat starts to settle in my spine. I wrap my legs around his hips, pulling him closer. The second his head hits my entrance, we both gasp, our eyes locking. And just as he opens his mouth to say something, I lift my hips, sending him plunging into my heat, making us both groan.

"Baby, shit...this feels..." I nod, knowing exactly what he means. It doesn't feel like the other times before. The warmth, the fullness, and the utter connection I feel with him surpass every feeling before. And it takes less than a second for both of us to realize why this time feels so much different.

"Condom," Owen growls as he moves to get up, but my legs wrap around his hips tighter, keeping him in place. His eyes come back to mine with questions swimming in their depths. "M?" I lean up, placing one of my hands on the side of his face as I kiss him gently, nipping his bottom lip until a groan escapes. I start to move my hips, his body visibly shaking against mine as I fuck him bare. I kiss his lips, across his jaw, and then nip the lobe of his ear.

"I'm on the pill," I whisper into the shell of his ear, feeling him shudder as my hips start grinding even harder, causing my head to fall back against the bed.

"You sure?" he asks, his eyes pleading with mine. I nod, needing him to move. The longer he stays inside me, the more I feel my walls contracting around him. He closes his eyes, leaning down and kissing me softly. "I love you," he says against my lips, kissing past my jaw and down my neck.

"I love you, too," I whimper, feeling his hips start to move.

"Say it again," he commands as he starts to fuck me slowly, moving in and out at a pace that drives me over the edge one thrust at a time.

"I love you," I repeat, wrapping my arms around his neck. That sets him off, and his hips start bucking against me, sending me spiraling toward an orgasm I didn't even know was there.

"Fuck, M, it's good to hear you say that. I never

thought I would hear it again," he admits, and for the first time in the last two days, I wonder what he's been through since all this started. Before I have a chance to ask, his cock hits me in a spot inside that sends stars bursting behind my eyelids, and I'm catapulted into an orgasm that far surpasses any I have ever had before.

"*Fuck…*" Owen utters, thrusting a few more times before I feel his cock expand, and he comes, his body locking above me.

He collapses, only rolling off when I tell him that he's cutting off my air supply. He chuckles as he gets up off the bed and heads into the bathroom on the other side of the room. When I hear the water running, I lay down, shutting my eyes, my arm coming over my face as my breathing starts to calm.

The feel of a warm cloth settling over my pussy startles me. When I look down my body, I'm left smiling at Owen, who stands above me, cleaning me up.

"You don't have to do that," I say, fully aware that I love him taking care of me.

"Nonsense, this is my job now. You are all I care about," he says as he throws the cloth back into the bathroom. It lands on the floor, and he settles in next to me once more.

As he pulls me toward him, my body tenses, thinking about the last time we did this. As if he read my mind, he kisses my temple and whispers, "I'm not going anywhere. There is nowhere I would rather be than with you, right here." I nod my head, laying my head on his chest, loving the sound of his heartbeat.

* * *

THE LIGHT from the bathroom wakes me as I hear Owen on the phone. When I look at the clock beside the bed, I see it's not even seven a.m. I groan, hugging his pillow closer as I settle again, waiting for him to come out. When he does, his eyes meet mine right away.

"Who was that?" I ask, my voice cracking with sleep. I yawn, loving the look in his eyes as he returns to the bed, pulling the pillow away from me and tugging me against him instead. This is what I missed last time—waking up to him against me, having him with me in the room. That's something I always knew I wanted but never expected to get.

"My lawyer," he states matter-of-factly. When I give him a look of confusion, he chuckles, and I feel it resonate through his entire body. "When I spent

the day trying to get those photos back from Bailey
—" My body locks at the mention of her name, but
he doesn't say anything about it. He just leans down
and kisses my temple and whispers, "I love you,"
before continuing. "Anyway, I threatened to call my
lawyer. So I'm just following through with that."

"Why would you threaten to call your lawyer?" I
ask, not really getting why he would bother when it's
all over.

"Just because you tell me it's not a big deal for
you, doesn't mean I feel the same. She violated you
in a way I can never take away." When I go to say
something, he shakes his head. "No, she did. She
took something that was meant only for me and
threatened to show anyone and everyone. I'm not
okay with that. Plus, she also tried to blackmail me
into breaking up with you. So, as of tomorrow, she's
being charged with blackmail unless she deletes all
evidence of those photos."

"Really?" I ask, loving the idea of those photos
not being in her hands any longer. Even though I
said I didn't really care if they were released, I would
really like to keep them just between us.

"Yes, really. I would never let her do anything to
hurt you, ever." I nod against his chest as he takes a
deep breath. "I'm also thinking of getting a

restraining order for both of us against her." Now that's a surprise. I lean up onto my elbow and look down at his face, seeing the seriousness of what he just said.

"You really think that's necessary?" I ask, not knowing if a piece of paper will stop her if she really wants to get close to us again.

"I need to know that you're protected. And knowing that she can't get near you will make me sleep easier at night. Plus, having her unable to get into the gym whenever she wants will be a nice change." I smile, feeling the laugh through his chest.

"If you think it's necessary, then we can go and sign the papers whenever you want," I say, noting the relief in his eyes.

"Thank you, baby." His hand grips the back of my neck, and he pulls me to his lips. When his tongue meets mine, everything I planned to talk about fades away, and all I can think about is how good he feels against me.

"I love you," he says, right before he pulls me on top of him, and I show him just how much I love him right back.

EPILOGUE

OWEN

"Can you just tell me where we're going?" Morgan asks as we drive down the coast. I've been planning this night for a year, and the fact that it's finally here makes my hands shake. I might drive us off the road if I don't hold onto the steering wheel hard enough.

"You know that's not how surprises work," I say, loving the earth-shattering smile she gives me as her head leans back against the seat of my truck, and her fingers twist with mine.

"Fine," she mutters, causing a small smile to cross my face as we continue on. There is nothing I wouldn't do for this woman, and I've told her that almost every day for the last year. After that day in New Orleans, I vowed never to do anything that would make her run again. And I've stayed true to that promise, no matter how many arguments we've had.

"Baby, it's your birthday. Can you please let me do this for you?" Out of the corner of my eye, I catch her looking at me. So, I turn my head, winking. She doesn't say anything, just sits back and lets me drive.

When we reach our destination, she sits up in her seat, her eyes wide as she looks from me to what's in front of her.

"How did you do this?" she asks, her voice a whisper as I bring her fingers to my lips and kiss them lightly. I say a silent prayer to her parents, who helped me set this up. Without them, I would never have been able to do it without Morgan figuring it out.

"Your parents love me," I say, giving her my best cocky smile as she rolls her eyes and gets out of the car. It's not a secret that they had some issues with me because of what happened last year, and still a little bit with our senior year of high school. But we all talked it out. Eventually, after months and months of proving to them that I wasn't going to hurt their daughter, they finally caved and started to love me.

"This is beautiful," she whispers as I take her

hand and lead her onto the beach, past the few people left lying in the setting sun, and head straight for our spot. I'm surprised she didn't know this is where we were headed. I didn't hide it, and yet the look on her face right now tells me that it was all worth it. Her eyes scan the area, taking in the white blanket sitting under the pier, the bottle of rosé that I know is her favorite sitting in a bucket of ice to the side, and a home-cooked meal—courtesy of her parents because, let's be honest, I can't cook to save my life.

"You did all this?" She turns and looks at me in awe, and I swear my heart stops right then. She looks so beautiful with her blond hair falling freely down to her shoulders, her eyes piercing me as I watch her take in every aspect of what's in front of her.

She's mine.

And in a few minutes, I'm hoping she'll be mine for a long, long time.

"M, baby, it's your birthday. Did you honestly think I wasn't going to do something?" There are instances, like right now, where I see a flash of uncertainty cross her face. A look that tells me she's still haunted by what happened last year. I won't sugarcoat anything and say it was a piece of cake after we came back home from New Orleans. It wasn't. Morgan and I spent months and months going to therapy, making sure we understood each other's desires and feelings and what it all meant to each of us and to us as a couple. I was never a big believer in therapy since I never had a reason to go, but it was important to Morgan, and therefore, it became important to me. It's still a work in progress, something I know we'll have to work at for the entirety of our relationship, but she's worth it. *We're* worth it, and every time I see that look cross her face, I walk toward her, cup her face in the palms of my hands and tell her exactly what she means to me. So, right now, I do exactly that.

"What are you doing?" she asks as I tilt her head back and look her directly in the eyes, smiling.

"You still have no idea, do you?" I whisper, taking her lips in a soft kiss that is supposed to last only a few seconds but turns heavy without me even trying. When we part, we're both breathing heavily, and I lean my forehead against hers and close my eyes, trying to catch my breath. "You still don't under-stand the magnitude with which I love you." She sucks in a breath as her fingers grasp the sides of my hands that are still cupping her gorgeous face. "Mor-gan, you are my life, the reason I breathe, the reason

I get up every morning with a smile on my face. This last year has been the best kind of wonderful, and when I came and got you in New Orleans, I made you a promise. I promised that I would spend the rest of my life making up for the fact that I made you question my love for you." She starts shaking her head, and it's in that moment that I sink down to one knee, holding her shaking hands in mine as I look up at the love of my life. She didn't know I planned to do this today. She also doesn't know there's a surprise party waiting for her at home with all her friends and family, including Allie and Ben, who flew in this morning.

"Owen, what are you doing?" Her eyes widen and she looks around us. All I can do is smile.

"I thought it would be pretty obvious," I tease, kissing the palm of each hand as tears stream down her face. "Morgan Lawson, you have been my best friend since we were twelve. There was never a day that went by that I didn't wish you were mine, even when we were apart. You were always my endgame." She smiles through her tears, and her hands start to shake as I grab the velvet box that's been burning a hole in my pocket for weeks. "I promised you that you would never have to doubt my love for you, and so I'm asking you—no, I'm begging you—to be my wife. Because I don't work without you." Her tears fall freely now, but she still says nothing. My heart starts to beat out of my chest. "M? Will you marry me?"

"Yes! Yes. Of course, I'll marry you!" she says, sinking to the blanket on the sand as I place the three-carat diamond ring on her finger, feeling my body settle, knowing that she's mine forever.

"I love you with everything I have," I whisper against her lips as her arms wrap around my neck.

"And I love you more than you know," she replies, kissing me twice before we part.

I couldn't ask for anything more than this moment.

She's everything.

My everything.

THE END.

WANT A FREE BOOK?

Join my newsletter and get a FREE copy of my short story Wounded Hearts! Join my Newsletter to get your copy!

WANT MORE SECOND CHANCE ROMANCE?

Check out Unauthorized Behaviour which is FREE in Kindle Unlimited!

ACKNOWLEDGMENTS

Thank you to my husband, who has stood by me throughout this journey. I know I can be hard to handle when deadlines hit, but your love and support will always mean the world to me.

Thank you to my family for supporting me no matter what I chose to do. They have always known that writing is my passion and seeing their support for that passion means everything to me.

Thank you to my BETA and ARC teams for reading my very rough drafts and telling me straight up what I need to change and how to create a better story. Thank you for sharing, loving and promoting my work. Without you, there would be no books to read and for that I am eternally grateful.

Thank you to Chelle. Thank you for taking me on, thank you for supporting me the way you have these past few months and thank you for elevating my work, it wouldn't be where it is today without you.

To my readers. When I started this journey, I

didn't know what to expect, and the level of love and support I've garnered over the last year has been something I never expected. You are the reason I do this job. You are the reason I write the stories I do, because you devour them and love them as much as I do. I hope that never changes.

ABOUT THE AUTHOR

S.A. Clayton lives in a small town outside of Toronto, Canada with her husband and her scary large collection of books that seem to take over every room.

She has worked on both sides of the publishing industry, both in a bookstore and for actual publishing companies. Although she loved both for different reasons, she found that writing was her true passion and has spent the last few years breaking into the industry as best she can.

She is a lover of all things romance and began her writing journey in her late twenties. Since then, she has immersed herself in the romance genre and couldn't be happier.

When she's not writing or reading, she enjoys binging a great Netflix show (Stranger Things anyone?), baking (because who doesn't love cookies!) and spending time with her family.

ALSO BY S.A. CLAYTON

Made in the USA
Coppell, TX
12 March 2022

74861412R00155